THE GUN WOLVES

A LONE MCGANTRY WESTERN

WAYNE D DUNDEE

The Gun Wolves
Paperback Edition

Wolfpack Publishing
5130 S. Fort Apache Rd. 215-380
Las Vegas, NV 89148

wolfpackpublishing.com

Paperback ISBN 978-1-63977-608-5
eBook ISBN 978-1-63977-511-8
LCCN 2022936952

THE GUN WOLVES

CHAPTER ONE

"FREEZE OR TAKE A BULLET!"

So went the command Lone McGantry issued to the rider passing through the shallow dry wash just a few feet below where Lone knelt in concealment on a stony ledge.

The rider responded promptly, halting his mount from continuing to pick its way along the rock-strewn floor of the gully twisting through these choppy hills on the western fringe of Nebraska's Pine Ridge region.

"That's right. Sit that saddle real still and keep those hands in plain sight," Lone advised. "I got a Winchester aimed at the top of your head and if you was to make a move that'd cause me to pull the trigger, what it would do to whatever's under your hat would be plumb messy."

Without moving or attempting to turn his head, the rider responded coolly, "My, that's a real surprise coming from of you, Mitchum—handing out a warning before you pull the trigger. You must be getting soft.

Way I heard, you always favored just hauling off and backshooting somebody to get it over and done with."

The surprise expressed by the rider wasn't without company. Lone felt the same thing upon hearing that the voice responding to him clearly belonged to a female. What the hell was going on?

"Lady," he drawled, "I don't know who you are or what you're up to, but you're ridin' a string of mistakes that damn near got your fool head blown off. For starters, you been foggin' my trail all morning and doin' a poor enough job of it for me to spot you and lag back to set this trap. And now you spout the name of some hombre that appears to make the whole thing all the more a wrong fit."

Edgily, over her shoulder, the rider in the gully said, "You saying you're not Turk Mitchum?"

"Never heard the name before in my life. You know what this Mitchum looks like?"

"Saw him once, briefly. Know him better from Wanted posters issued against him."

Lone paused for a beat. Then, rising up from the clump of bramble he'd been crouched behind, still keeping his Winchester Yellowboy aimed steady, he said, "All right. Real slow and makin' sure to keep those hands empty and in plain sight, turn around and have a look."

Below him, the rider did as instructed. Twisting slowly at the waist, raising one hand with equal slowness to push a spill of thick chestnut hair back behind her ear, the girl lifted her face to gaze up. Her appraisal of Lone brought no change to her expression. He, in return, had to fight to keep his own expression from displaying a reaction to her striking beauty.

"Well," Lone said after their eyes had locked for a long moment, "am I Mitchum—the man you thought you were following?"

"No," the girl responded measuredly. "No, you're not."

Lone nodded. "Okay. Good, we've got that much settled. So what caused you, then, to latch on to my trail thinkin' I *was* him?"

"Your tracks. The horse you're riding has a right forefoot canted slightly outward. Those are the tracks of the horse Mitchum was riding when he left Newbridge four days ago." The girl's gaze turned into a scowl. "So that leads to a question I have for you: What are you doing riding Turk Mitchum's horse?"

Lone considered for a minute before stating, "Appears this is gonna take some jawboning to sort out all the way. Before we get to that, shuck your gunbelt and drop it on the off side of your horse. Then you step down on this side and hold steady, still keepin' those hands in plain sight and in front of you until I climb down from here. Remember, this Winchester will be trained on you the whole while."

Even as she complied with his instructions, a corner of the girl's mouth quirked up somewhat smugly and she said, "You're an awful cautious character, aren't you?"

"Been my experience it pays to be that way," Lone told her as he made his way down from the ledge.

Reaching the floor of the gully, he quickly saw that closer examination did nothing to diminish the initial impact of the girl before him. Her face was a perfect oval framed by a mane of lustrous reddish brown hair tumbling down from a flat-crowned tan Stetson. The face was highlighted by bold dark eyes, high cheekbones, and a wide, lush mouth. Below that, abundant womanly curves were well displayed in snug corduroy pants, a wine-colored shirt, and a tobacco brown vest worn unbuttoned in a way that accentuated the swell of high, proud breasts.

"Well?" said the girl, eyeing him challengingly after he'd finished his appraisal. "Are you going to answer me about how you come to be riding Mitchum's horse?"

"We'll get to that," Lone replied. "But first, have you got a name? And how is it you come to be trackin' this Mitchum jasper anyway?"

"My name is Velda Beloit. I'm a bounty hunter and, like I said, Mitchum has Wanted dodgers on him. That makes him my business. I've got one of the handbills issued on him in my vest pocket. If you don't get too anxious with that Winchester, I can show it to you."

Lone nodded. "Go ahead."

Velda slowly took a folded piece of paper from her pocket, shook it open to indeed reveal a handbill, held it up for Lone to examine.

He did so with quick flicks of his eyes, never taking them off the girl for very long at a time. When he was satisfied, he gave another short nod. "Okay, it's as you say. And the droopy eyes, weak chin—yeah, it's the same hombre I ran into." Then, as the paper was refolded and returned to the vest pocket, he said, "So you're a bounty hunter, eh?"

"That's right. You can spare me any remarks, I've heard them all." Her dark eyes narrowed. "Now how about you—you got a name?"

"Make it McGantry. Lone McGantry."

"Lone?"

"It's a long story but, yeah, Lone is how it shakes out."

Now Lone felt those dark eyes making an appraisal of him. What they saw was a tall, broad-shouldered hombre a ways past the forty mark. A battered, dust- and sweat-streaked Stetson rode atop a squarish, weathered face anchored by a prominent nose and alert, flinty eyes. Standard trail garb of faded denims, boiled white shirt, buckskin vest; Colt holstered on his right hip, Bowie knife sheathed on his left. In short, not a man looking to court trouble but neither one to walk too wide around it.

When he figured he'd been sufficiently sized up, Lone flashed a tolerant half-grin and said, "Which brings us right back around to the question of me and Mitchum's horse. Right?"

"I think it still deserves an answer."

Lone sighed. "Yeah, reckon it does."

"Do you have to keep holding that rifle on me to tell it?"

Lone gave it a beat and then lowered the muzzle of the Yellowboy. Twisting his mouth ruefully, he said, "Despite my brag about always bein' cautious, it pains me greatly to admit that a failure to do so regardin' your man Mitchum pretty much tells the story on how I ended up with his horse. You see, he showed up at my camp three nights ago, just ahead of that big storm that passed through. Had a sad tale about bein' a drifter down on his luck, complete with a lame horse. I could see the part about the horse was true by the way the animal was stepping when he walked it in. Looked like a pulled front shoulder muscle.

"My only excuse for lowerin' my guard is that I'm a

sucker for ailing horses. More so than people, comes right down to it. Plus I have a kind of knack for sometimes helping critters in misery. So that's what I was doin', after I allowed Mitchum into camp and told him to help himself to some coffee I was leanin' over to examine the horse's cramped shoulder to see if I might be able to do anything for it. That's when I got clubbed from behind. Knocked colder than a wedge. Didn't come back around until the rain started in. Found the dry-gulchin' skunk long gone on my horse, and me left with his lame one."

"It's a wonder he left you alive," Velda said, her expression grim.

"Guess he figured I wasn't worth a bullet. Or maybe he was showin' his gratitude for the coffee."

"You saw the list of charges on that handbill. Mitchum has never shown any reluctance to burn through bullets and he didn't come to be known as 'Murderin' Mitchum' by showing mercy for any reason."

Lone cocked one eyebrow. "You almost sound like you're disappointed he *didn't* kill me."

"It's just curious, that's all. He starts acting out of character, could mark a change that'll make it even harder to run down the foul dog."

"Maybe so. But remember there's one other change you can count on for certain."

"What's that?"

"Me. I'm in the mix now. On top of whatever else Mitchum has done, he made the mistake of stealin' my horse—and I mean to get it back from the sonofabitch."

CHAPTER TWO

AFTER RETRIEVING HER GUNBELT, VELDA BELOIT TOOK her horse by its reins and walked with Lone farther down the gully to where he'd stashed his own mount before doubling back to take up the high position from which he'd gotten the drop on her. As they walked, they continued to talk. Though later on neither might have been able to say (or perhaps admit) who brought it up, it wasn't long before the notion of possibly joining forces in the pursuit of Turk Mitchum entered into the discussion.

"I'm not out to horn in on your bounty," Lone assured her. "All I want is my horse back. Me and that big old gray—I call him Ironsides, by the way—have been through too much together for me to give him up easy. And, since those Wanted papers on Mitchum say Dead or Alive, if it happens I have to drill him full of holes in order to get the job done, then that won't cost you neither."

Velda eyed him. "Sounds to me like a lopsided

arrangement for you. But if that's how you want to work it, I'd be a fool to argue. Especially if Mitchum is on his way to where I got a hunch he might be headed. If I'm right, then anybody going in after him would be smart to have some backup."

Lone said, "Where is it you figure he's headed?"

"Remember it's just a hunch," Velda reminded him. "Until I could be sure is why I stuck with tailing him—or what I thought was him. Like I said, I picked up his trail back in Newbridge. But then I lost it after that frog strangler of a storm the other night. I went on for a while, moving in the direction of my hunch. I didn't like the uncertainty of that, though, so I doubled back and began riding in wide side to side sweeps, hoping to pick up some fresh sign. That's how I came upon what you were leaving and was glad, at least for a little while, that I'd gone to the extra trouble because the direction had changed to the south instead of northwest like before."

"Only now that it's turned out to be me leavin' the sign," Lone concluded with a wry twist of his mouth, "you're thinkin' Mitchum likely stuck with continuin' the way he had been."

"Seems reasonable, don't you think?"

"Probably our best bet," Lone allowed. "Havin' no idea which way Mitchum came from when he showed up at my camp and damn sure none on which way he went when he left, I was just makin' a guess by strikin' south. Like you, I had no trail to follow on account of the storm. So I reckoned south was the way I'd sooner encounter some ranches or towns where I might find somebody who'd remember spotting the horse thievin' wretch."

By this point they had reached the grulla horse

formerly belonging to Mitchum, where Lone had left it tied to a bush on a shoulder of the dry wash. Giving the animal a close looking over, Velda said with a hint of concern, "Is this nag going to hold up after that shoulder problem?"

"He's been doin' okay so far," Lone told her. "Though I've only been riding him part of yesterday and so far today, and not pushin' him too hard. Didn't even try takin' him out of camp right away. I spent a day and a half treatin' that shoulder. Like I said, I got a kind of knack when it comes to tending ailin' critters. Luckily, Mitchum left behind my saddle and gear and in my possibles I have a bottle of good liniment that I used while givin' this old grulla regular rubdowns to loosen up that cramped muscle.

"By the end of the first day I could feel it workin' and I began walking him in easy circles, first turnin' one way and then the other. By the middle of yesterday he appeared to be steppin' pretty good so I saddled him up and rode out the afternoon. I picked easy trails and didn't push too hard and he held up well. I treated him last night and again this morning and so far so good. Can't say I'd count on him for outrunning a pack of howlin' Injuns, but I figure he'll get me far enough to where I can make a trade. From there, the next thing will be getting to where I can put my saddle back on Ironsides again."

For the first time, Velda showed a genuine though brief smile. "You're sure fond of that big gray, aren't you?"

"Me and him been together a long time. Been through some rough patches together, and I could always count on him." Lone's expression darkened for a moment. "I've never been close to very many people and some of the ones I was, I lost in recent times. I don't mean for Ironsides to fall into that same category."

"I'm sorry I brought up unpleasant memories," Velda said earnestly.

Lone shook his head. "Ain't unpleasant memories we need to be worried about. Where our focus belongs is on a current pile of unpleasantness by the name of Mitchum. So what about this place you got a hunch he might be makin' tracks for?"

THEY RODE northwest through the balance of the day. The summer sun was hot, though not brutal, so they held to a steady pace without pushing the grulla too hard. As they rode, the terrain they passed through changed—drastically at first, as the Pine Ridge escarpment fell away, and then more gradually until most scatterings of smaller rock outcrops also disappeared. Beyond that the choppy, tree-sprinkled hills of taller grass smoothed out, grew more blunted, and became covered by the beginnings of the short grass prairie.

As sundown approached, they crossed the Niobrara River near its upper reach and entered into Wyoming. For night camp they selected a flat clearing tucked within a curving line of cottonwoods and aspens.

While Lone tended the horses, including another quick liniment rubdown of the grulla's shoulder, Velda got a fire going and set a pot of coffee to brew. Walking over to join her at the fire, Lone said, "I sure hope we land some place where I can find some more of that liniment. It's good stuff to keep on hand, but I'm usin' up most of my supply on that grulla."

"Whether it's the liniment or your rubdown technique, something seems to be working pretty good," Velda responded. "My first impression of that critter was that he might not be able to *stand* all day, let alone carry a rider over a stretch of miles. But he stayed with it the whole while."

Holding up his hands and taking a whiff of the stinging liniment odor still clinging to them, Lone said, "Maybe it's the smell of the liniment that does all the work. It's mighty potent. Maybe the fumes make the animal so drunk they're sorta numb to whatever pain they're in."

"In that case, maybe you'd better go wash your hands before you intoxicate the both of us."

"Apart from that risk, neither is it exactly an appetizin' smell to go with grub."

Lone went over to where his saddle lay, knelt down and first sand-washed his hands. Then he took a bar of soap from his saddlebags, wet his hands with sloshes of tepid water from his canteen and worked up a good lather before rinsing them off. Turning back to Velda, wiping his palms on his shirt, he announced, "There. Now I smell like lilacs. Leastways that's what the barber who sold me that bar of soap promised it would do."

"Well it's definitely an improvement on the liniment, I can attest to that," Velda said with a smile. Then, the smile taking on a somewhat rueful twist, she added, "Unfortunately, that doesn't mean the improved smell will directly improve the grub, as you call it. Not if I'm the cook, that is. I guess I should have warned you...I make a mean pot of coffee but most anything else I've ever attempted to cook has turned out so bad I gave up trying."

"To ride around the country chasin' down owlhoots, it must take something more than coffee to keep you going."

"In my possibles pack," Velda told him, "you'll find a good supply of beef jerky and several airtights of canned peaches. That does the trick for me. At least until I reach a town with a good restaurant or cafe—then I make up the difference by putting a serious dent in whatever's on the menu."

Lone said, "Still and all, a body can go a long way on coffee and jerky. Maybe some hardtack. Though canned peaches, I gotta admit, sound like a mighty tasty add-on."

"Certainly more so than hardtack. Ugh." Velda made a face. "I tried some of that from my father's pack once and it was awful. Tasted like burnt sand and was as hard as chewing on a rock. Heck, even my bad cooking wouldn't stack up so bad."

Lone grinned. "That's why soldiers call hardtack biscuits 'tooth dullers'. In a pinch, though, they make do as belly fillers. Back when I was scoutin' for the army during the thick of the Indian trouble and sometimes found myself off alone where I had to settle for a cold night camp because I couldn't risk a campfire, I took many a meal made up of jerky and hardtack washed down by canteen water."

During the course of the afternoon, Lone and Velda had filled each other in on their respective backgrounds. Lone told how, as an infant, he was the only survivor of an Indian raid. He grew up being raised by the army wives at Fort McPherson and, though his parents' surname was known to have been McGantry, there was no record ever found of what they'd named their child. Hence, the subsequent frequent references to him as "the lone McGantry" who survived the massacre eventually got shortened and simply "Lone" became what he was called. It stuck with him as he grew to manhood and went on, among other things, to serve as an army scout.

For her part, Velda related her path to becoming a bounty hunter as resulting from being the only child of a widower Kansas sheriff who taught her the skills of riding, shooting, and tracking over more standard "girly stuff". This led to her becoming his chief deputy by the time she was twenty—just a few months before her father was gunned down and killed from ambush. When Velda went after his killers only to meet with what she perceived as hindrance from terms like "jurisdiction" and "due process", she threw away her badge and delivered justice on her terms. Taking up bounty work and pursuing fugitives who managed to elude capture often due to similar legal constraints, was how she'd been making her way ever since.

Befitting his name, Lone had never been one to feel at ease around a stranger until a considerable amount of favorable exposure had come to pass. Even then, the number of regular acquaintances he tended to tolerate was small and those he counted as genuine friends were even scarcer. Yet for all that, by the close of the afternoon he found himself beginning to feel quite at ease in the presence of Velda. Having a common enemy no doubt explained part of it. Another reason, he reckoned, was that her tale of tragedy and grit was something he could relate to. And then, of course, her striking beauty wasn't exactly a trait to drive a man away.

As much as anything perhaps was the fact Lone had just come off a long, reflective stretch of purposely keeping even more apart from other people than usual. Though he'd probably be too stubborn to admit it, this possibly had him more open to a new acquaintance then he might otherwise be. Plus, again, the fact said acquaintance was so pleasing to look at surely didn't hurt.

"So what I'm hearin'," he said now, summing up their discussion of meal options, "is that if I want anything more than coffee, jerky, and maybe some of your peaches, I'd better break out my own frying pan and something to put in it. That about right?"

"Sounds like," Velda agreed. "And if I'm willing to share my peaches, does that mean you're willing to share what comes out of your pan?"

"Seems fair. But keep in mind I'm not talkin' anything fancier than bacon and beans," Lone advised her.

"Sounds fancy enough for me."

"Done deal, then. While I'm cookin', you can tell me some more about this town of Pickaxe we're planning to visit."

Velda's brow wrinkled. "I don't really know what else to add. I've never been there, I've just heard the stories. Those stories make it a place I'd normally want to steer clear of. But, at the same time, they make Pickaxe a perfect fit for Mitchum. And since every indication seems to be that's where he's headed...well, I don't aim to let no town's reputation get in the way of going ahead and running down a cur I've set my sights on."

A corner of Lone's mouth quirked up in a crooked smile as he began slicing strips of bacon and laying them out in an oversized frying pan. Once again the girl's words indicated the kind of grit and determination that he found so appealing.

CHAPTER THREE

From what Velda related, Lone learned that Pickaxe was a former boom town located south of the Devil's Tower region in upper northeast Wyoming. Like many such places, it had sprung up fast and sprawling and boisterous on the promise of an initial gold strike turning into more rich deposits for any who came to bust them out of the ground. But while a few additional deposits did get found, they weren't that rich or that numerous. Almost as fast as it had sprung to life, Pickaxe (so named due to the old prospector who found the first gold throwing down his pickaxe in disgust and frustration after another day of coming up empty, only to have the discarded tool accidentally split open a rock and reveal a flash of the precious color he'd so desperately been searching for) emptied out and became a leftover sprawl of hastily constructed buildings discarded in much the same way as the instrument that had spawned it.

If not for a handful of stubborn hangers-on, the place would have become another ghost town inhabited by nothing but the unforgiving elements. Those who remained managed to get by from continuing to peck out meager bits of gold with which they made periodic trips to where they could turn it into cash. They also did some trading with the local Indian tribes, did a little farming and tending of small cattle and goat herds, and offered lodging and meals to the occasional traveler who drifted through.

It was one such traveler, a hardcase called Lobo Hines, who saw possibilities in Pickaxe far removed from anything the town had represented before then. He envisioned how riches could once again be made here. Not from gold, at least not the kind you had to scrape and dig out of the ground, but in other ways. Hines had long ago decided that a man with brains and guts and the right kind of persuasive techniques could line his pockets very nicely from the toil of others, not from breaking a sweat himself.

A few weeks later, when Lobo Hines showed up in Pickaxe a second time, he was riding at the head of a dozen other men, all hard bitten cusses cut from similar cloth as him. With them, they brought a string of pack animals heavily laden with supplies. Upon arrival, Hines called together the existing residents of the town and announced that he and his men were taking over. He was the self-appointed mayor, his men should be considered a combination city council and enforcers of the new rules that would govern Pickaxe going forward.

The town was to be revitalized with new businesses to include, for starters, a saloon, general store, and hotel. Patronage for these establishments would come from those attracted by word already widely spread by Hines and his men—for a price and for adherence to the rules laid out by the enforcement committee, Pickaxe would serve as a safe haven for owlhoots or fugitives of any stripe looking to lay low for a while and be shielded from pursuit.

The citizens already present got told they were welcome to remain and continue living as they were, as long as they obeyed the new rules and made no attempt to otherwise interfere with the changes. What was more, as soon as the new businesses were up and running, they would represent employment opportunities for any who wanted increased earnings to what they were currently scraping by on.

Nobody really knew how many of the citizens on hand that first day adapted or survived, but the revised Pickaxe—as not only a safe haven but also a kind of headquarters for the plotting and execution of new criminal activity—thrived and grew beyond even what Lobo Hines had imagined. Backed by his enforcement committee, who came to be known as the Gun Wolves, he kept a close eye and a tight grip on everything and took a generous cut from all that transpired.

"No law dogs ride herd on any of this?" Lone questioned.

"What law? There is none up that way, except what a town provides for itself. In the case of Pickaxe, that means only Lobo's Gun Wolves and the rules they enforce." Velda huffed sarcastically. "Otherwise, it's outside the jurisdiction—there's one of my favorite words again—of any standard law enforcement outfit."

"What about federal marshals?"

Velda shrugged. "There've been reports of one or two U.S. Marshals riding in looking for specific owlhoots they were on the trail of. But they came out empty handed. Lobo has a good sniffer for detecting newcomers who don't rate the welcome mat getting rolled out for 'em. And he's mighty careful about hiding any person or activity he doesn't want seen until he's sure a newcomer passes the smell test. Those who don't, are strongly encouraged to keep on riding. If they fail to take the hint...well, they seem not to be heard from anymore."

"I can see," Lone said as he stirred the small pot of beans he'd placed on the coals beside the frying pan, "why you call it a place you'd sooner steer clear of. How long before we reach it?"

"About a day and a half, I figure. There's a town called Lusk in between. Expect we'll pass through there around mid-day tomorrow."

"Any chance of us catchin' up with Mitchum before then?"

Velda shook her head. "Not likely. I lost too much time backtracking to try and pick up his trail again but then getting misled by the one you left instead. I expect Mitchum is probably in Pickaxe by now."

"Meanin' we're gonna have to go in after him." Lone twisted his mouth wryly. "Comes to that, what do you figure our chances are for passin' Lobo's smell test?"

"Better for me than you."

"Oh? How so?"

"I didn't mean to sound smug, but it's something I already had a rough plan for before the two of us threw in together," Velda explained. "Word has it, you see, that Lobo is always on the lookout for girls to work in his saloons. If I say so myself, was I to trade my gunbelt and britches for a dress, pin up my hair and maybe pat on some face powder, I figure I'd be eye pleasing enough for a pack of rowdy, half-drunk law dodgers. Plus, if I show enough leg to offset any sour notes I might hit, I make a pretty fair singer-dancer."

Lone frowned. "Sounds to me like a plan that would put you in a mighty risky position."

"I've been in them before. And I've made that saloon entertainer disguise work before, too. I know how to handle myself," Velda assured him.

"What about Mitchum, if you go paradin' around in Lobo's saloons? Ain't he apt to recognize you?"

Velda gave another shake of her head. "He's never laid eyes on me. Like I said, I caught a glimpse of him once but it was from an upstairs window. He never looked my way. He knows there are plenty of bounty hunters and lawmen after him, but he'd have no idea I'm one of 'em. To help make sure, I'll use phony name to go with my saloon girl act."

"Sounds like you got it all figured pretty tight."

"What about you? Mitchum was in your camp long enough for a cup of coffee before he conked you over the head. Won't he recognize you?"

Lone considered a minute. "It was dark, meager light from the campfire. We didn't palaver much before I bent over to take a look at the grulla's shoulder...Me showin' up in an unexpected place after this amount of time has passed, no, I don't think there's much risk he'd know who I was."

"But not zero risk, either."

"Not much about what we've set out to do is free of some degree of risk." Lone paused for a moment, pressing his lips into a tight, straight line. Then: "But I still say puttin' yourself in the role of a saloon floozy is more of one than necessary."

"Saloon *entertainer*, not 'floozy' thank you. Don't worry, I can handle it. Of more concern is you not getting the unwelcome treatment. If you're able to stick around for a while, then let's accept we'll both be in risky positions but at least it will give us the chance to watch each other's back."

"Just the two of us against a whole pack of gunslicks and cutthroats is gonna take a powerful lot of back watchin'," Lone allowed somewhat grimly. "But, like you, I've had the odds stacked against me before. And if goin' into Pickaxe is what I got to do to get my horse back, then I'll have to come up with an idea for makin' myself welcome at least long enough to get the job done."

"And also the job of taking down the murderous skunk who stole him," Velda tossed in as a reminder.

Lone nodded. "Don't worry, I'll help you make sure that part gets taken care of too...Now hold out your plate, I'll scoop on some beans and stab you three or four strips of bacon. While we eat, we can also chew on some ideas for gettin' me past Lobo's smell test."

CHAPTER FOUR

THEY'D RIDDEN FOR A LITTLE OVER TWO HOURS THE following morning when Lone reined his mount closer alongside Velda and said, "In case you haven't noticed, we have some riders comin' up behind us. I make it three, about a quarter mile back."

Without turning to look, Velda asked, "Are they following us?"

"Can't tell for sure. Could be they're just on the same course. They don't appear to be pushin' overly hard but the pace we're setting, remember, is pretty tame. All things stay the same, they're bound to overtake us before too long."

"What do you suggest?"

"Well, even if we wanted to, we ain't fixed to outrun 'em. Not with this grulla," Lone said. "Seems to me our best play would be to find a spot favorable to us and then call a halt, wait for 'em to catch up, see what's on their minds."

"Speaking of the grulla, needing to pay some attention to his shoulder could give us a reasonable excuse for stopping," Velda suggested. "It wouldn't seem suspicious if you were rubbing in some more of that liniment when they showed."

Lone nodded. "Good idea. That's how we'll set it up then."

The terrain had changed some more over the course of the morning. Many of the smooth, gently blunted hills were now taking on sharper crests and stands of aspen and cottonwoods, though scattered, were becoming more common. Rising up like oversized tombstones at the ends of some of the sharply-crested hills, short lengths of flat-faced, redstone cliffs had also begun appearing with increased frequency.

It was against the face of one of these cliffs, with the weather-pitted reddish stone standing like a wall at their backs and the slopes of the hill falling away to a clear field of vision in three directions, that Lone signaled a halt. They took their time watering their horses out of their hats and then Lone broke out his bottle of liniment. All the while, he and Velda monitored the approach of the three riders as they rose and fell from sight passing over and between the intervening hills.

When they were finally ascending the slope of the hill where Lone and Velda waited, they revealed themselves to be a mixed bag not uncommon to the remote trails of the unsettled West. They might represent menace or they might be just three shiftless hombres looking for a place to earn their next grub stake.

The gent riding at the center of the trio was a stocky, square-shouldered individual on the plus side of forty. He had a broad, flat face bracketed by bushy sideburns extending from under a battered, wide-brimmed hat.

His attire consisted of a homespun collarless shirt worn untucked over striped pants stuffed into scuffed, mud-spattered boots. A gunbelt was cinched around his plentiful waist and a converted Navy Colt rode high in a holster rigged for the cross draw.

To his left rode another man of similar age and attire. His hat was somewhat less battered and a stubborn spill of gray-flecked hair dangled across his broad forehead. His eyes were set too close on either side of a thick, wide-nostriled nose that appeared to have been broken more than once. He too wore a gunbelt with his shooting iron holstered for the cross draw.

The remaining rider was a dozen or so years younger than his companions, leaner and better dressed. He wore a black leather vest with silver conchos for buttons. A bowler hat sat atop his narrow, sharp-eyed face and long tendrils of greasy dark hair spilled down in front of his ears and over the back of his neck. His gunbelt was also of black leather, sporting twin holsters packed with matching ivory-handled Colts.

Lone's closer, lengthier assessment of the three was that they obviously weren't drifters looking for common labor, but rather hardcases who were no strangers to crowding—and likely stepping over at times—the boundaries of the law. Assessing further, he reckoned that the younger man with the showy two-gun rig was probably fast and dangerous in his own right but, if push came to shove, it would be one of the two older dogs Lone would aim to take a bite out of first.

"Mornin' to ya," sang out the middle rider, the one with the bushy sideburns. "I'll hold off sayin' *good* mornin' on account of it looks like you maybe got some trouble with your animal there."

Straightening up from where he'd been unnecessarily applying a fresh dab of liniment to the grulla's shoulder, Lone wiped his hands on a rag and replied, "Nothing overly serious. Critter pulled a muscle a while back and I been rubbin' it down regular to keep it loosened up until I can get him somewhere I can work a swap."

Bushy Sideburns studied him. "Uh-huh. Guess that explains why you been travelin' so slow, eh? We spotted your campfire smoke at first light and then saw you pokin' along up ahead, same way we was aimed."

"Yeah, we been taking it a little easy," Lone allowed. "Understand there's a town called Lusk not too much farther up ahead."

"Yeah, Lusk is there. But how do you figure to make a deal on a lame nag?" sneered the fellow with the close set eyes. "Wouldn't hardly be on the up and up to sucker some poor fool like that, would it?"

Keeping his voice calm and level, Lone said, "Wouldn't try to hide the shoulder trouble. Couldn't if I wanted to. But that don't make the animal lame permanent-like. A little extra care and some pasture time to all the way heal, he'll be good as new. But since I'm lookin' to stay on the move, I don't have that kind of time to spend."

"Where you and your gal friend on the move to?" asked Bushy Sideburns.

Lone gave it a long beat, signaling he didn't care much for the probing. Then, in a measured tone, he said, "We're workin' on more of a direction than what you might call a firm destination. Montana high country has been spoke of, if nothing more interestin' crops up along the way."

"Whew! Montana, now that's quite a stretch of miles. Rough country and plenty of rough customers to be found in it." Bushy Sideburns frowned. "Mighty rugged undertakin' to be haulin' such a pretty young thing along on."

Velda, who had been standing quiet up until then, was moved to respond somewhat tartly, "For your information, mister, nobody is *hauling* me anywhere. McGantry and I may be traveling together but I'm quite capable of handling rugged country on my own if need be."

This brought an exaggerated groan out of the bowler-hatted young man. "Now you went and did it, Harley. You done offended the little lady. Dang, here I was thinking we maybe oughta start lookin' to find ourselves a pretty travelin' partner like her. But if you're gonna right away say the wrong thing to piss 'em off, ain't none gonna last very long, are they?"

"Maybe it's you who'd better worry about sayin' the wrong thing, Seth boy," warned Close Eyes.

"Aw, he was just funnin' some, Mort. Don't be so quick to get your hackles up," advised the one addressed as Harley. "And speakin' of raisin' hackles, maybe I owe an apology to the lady for givin' short shrift to her abilities."

"Apologize if you want," muttered Mort, "but I didn't hear no harm in what you said. Fact is, a body don't see many gals tough enough to strike out for such a long, hard way from the seat of a saddle."

"You don't see many gals packin' a shootin' iron on their waist and makin' it look right at home there, neither," pointed out Harley. Then, aiming his words directly at Velda now, he added, "You clearly are a woman of bravery and grit, ma'am, and I'm honored to meet you. If my pards and I have barged in rudely and been discourteous with our words, I apologize on the part of all of us."

"That's not necessary," Velda told him. "Perhaps I was overly testy."

"You're too gracious. In case you didn't catch it, my name is Harley. My pals here are Mort and" —gesturing to indicate each man respectively— "the sprout of our bunch, Seth."

Though not formed as another question, the self-introduction by Harley was clearly meant for Lone and Velda to respond in kind. Before Lone could speak up, Velda quickly said, "This is McGantry. My name is Roxie Drew."

Velda's use of a phony name was obviously meant as a warning of some kind to Lone, but he wasn't sure what. With the three riders now reined up so close, there was no chance for her to express anything more distinct with words or even with her eyes. Lone's own read of the men already had him on guard, now he became even more so.

"There now," declared Harley. "The trail out in these empty stretches can be such a lonely place that I always like to say howdy and trade names whenever I run into a stranger. It's only civil, don't you think? A-course pokin' any more than that...like askin' what business a body might have for bein' out in all this lonely...that'd be pushin' too far."

"Way most people see it," Lone agreed.

Harley leaned forward, resting his forearm atop his

saddle horn, and heaved a sigh. "On the other hand, was a person to run across somebody they had reason to suspicion was a lowdown skunk and a crook, then in that case I believe they'd have not only a right but an obligation to do some holdin' to account. What do you say to that?"

"I'd say," Lone replied, "that you got a mighty long-winded way of tryin' to make some kind of point. Then I'd say why don't you just go ahead and spit it the hell out of your craw and get it over with?"

Harley's eyes narrowed and turned flinty as he pushed himself back erect in his saddle. "Alright, bub. Here's what's in my craw...I damned quick want an answer to what you're doin' ridin' Turk Mitchum's grulla horse?"

CHAPTER FIVE

TENSION SUDDENLY GRIPPED THE HILLTOP AND ALL gathered there like a clenched fist. Lone cut a quick glance over at Velda. When he swung his eyes back to Harley, he saw that Mort and Seth were also nailing him with hard glares.

Forming his own scowl, Lone said, "Turk Mitchum, eh? So that's the horse thievin' bastard's name. Thanks, you've given me more to go on than I had up to now. What else can you tell me about him?"

Harley's glare fell away, replaced by a half surprised, half confused expression. "What? Wait a minute—I'm the one askin' the questions here. Where do you get off callin' somebody else a horse thief when you're the one in possession of another man's hayburner?"

"The *reason* I'm in possession of this gimpy hayburner," Lone grated through clenched teeth, "is because his former owner—this Mitchum, you call him—didn't give me no damn choice. He showed up in my camp some nights back, walkin' with this lame grulla in tow. Suckered me with a sad tale and then, as soon as I wasn't looking, walloped me from behind and left me knocked cold. When I woke up, Mitchum and my big healthy stud were long gone and I was left with this sorry critter. Took me until yesterday to get the shoulder in good enough shape to head out on the trail again."

Under a skeptically arched brow, the one called Seth said, "That's a mighty serious claim—callin' a fella a horse thief."

"Ain't that what your pal Harley just accused me of?" Lone countered.

"I said what I had to say to your face," responded Harley. "Mitchum ain't nowhere around to defend himself."

"Fair enough. Tell me where to find him," said Lone, "I'll gladly call him a horse thief to his face!"

"We ain't hardly in the habit of spillin' about a friend to every tough-talkin' stranger who comes down the pike," growled Mort.

"So you admit that Mitchum is a friend of yours, is that it?" Velda demanded sharply. "If that's the case, why aren't you riding with him?"

Before Mort could answer, Harley said, "We got a lot of friends we don't ride steady with. Happens we ran into Mitchum a week or so back but at the time had some separate business to take care of. We been figurin' to join up with him again a ways down the trail...Now what's your story on this big hombre you're ridin' with? Was you there when Mitchum swapped horses the way he claims?"

Velda shook he head. "Not that it's any of your business but no, we didn't meet up until later. Found out we were headed in the same direction, decided to ride together for a ways. Simple as that."

"Kinda risky for a lone gal to throw in with such a rough-around-the-edges character, don't you think? Real careless habit to form, you want my advice."

"I don't, particularly," Velda replied in a frosty tone. "But I'll give you some in return. Since you and your pal Mort seem so worried about bad habits, then one of your own you ought to change in a hurry is not being so careless when it comes to choosing friends like Turk Mitchum."

"Whether you want it or not," huffed Mort, "here's another piece of advice, and one you'd best take real serious: Learn not to stick you pretty nose in or shoot off your sassy mouth where unwelcome—else it might earn you a lesson that won't leave you so pretty no more!"

"Now hold on," protested Seth. "One bad habit we *don't* have is roughin' up women. Especially not pretty ones like this." He paused, his mouth spreading in a wide, lewd grin before adding, "So how about I take Miss Sassy here off to one side and gentle her down some...While you two go ahead and teach a lesson to this nasty horse thief she was unfortunate enough to fall in the clutches of?"

Before either Harley or Mort could say anything, Velda herself replied in what sounded, at first, like a conciliatory tone. "I've got a better idea. How about I go willingly with all three of you...To the nearest sheriff's office, where I can turn the lot of you in for the bounties issued on your otherwise worthless hides!" With those closing words, the frostiness returned to Velda's voice and at the same time the Colt previously riding on her hip was suddenly in her fist and aimed at the three horsemen bunched before her.

There was a clock tick of indecision on the parts of

Harley, Mort, and Seth. Looking on, Lone could see it in their eyes, read the thoughts squirming in their twisted brains. Their three guns against one, they were thinking —and that in the hand of a woman. So focused, so furiously affronted were they by this that they momentarily forgot all about him.

He tried to warn them, grating "Don't try it, boys" even as his hand was closing around the grips of his own Colt.

But there was no stopping it. The three hardcases couldn't accept that they were somehow at a disadvantage.

Harley set it in motion, bellowing, "To hell with you, bitch!" as his meaty paw slapped down on the converted Navy. Simultaneously, Mort and Seth released their reins and also grabbed for iron.

Velda didn't hesitate. Her already drawn gun roared and spat flame. Just as Lone had done earlier, she assessed that the greater threat was posed by the two veteran hardcases over mouthy, flashy young Seth. So, she aimed her first round at Harley, striking him high on his torso halfway between collarbone and the ball of his left shoulder. The impact jolted the big man, twisting him partly around so that his reaching hand failed to close properly on the grips of the Navy. It was the only chance he got. Velda's second shot, quickly adjusted, drilled a slug into the base of Harley's throat a fraction of an inch below his Adam's apple. His head snapped back and he emitted a kind of gargling squawk just ahead of toppling to the ground.

Meanwhile, Mort succeeded in getting his gun unleathered. But before he could level it and try to take aim, Lone's Colt was bucking in his fist and sending a heart-rupturing, life-ending bullet to the left center of Mort's chest. The gun that had cleared its holster slipped from lifeless fingers and dropped off one side of the horse while Mort's sagging body tipped and fell the opposite way.

This left only Seth who, despite limited expectations from both Lone and Velda, demonstrated lightning speed at drawing his brace of shiny pistols. From there, however—perhaps rattled by the sight of his two companions biting the dust—his follow-through proved wild and inaccurate. He snapped off hurried shots from a gun in each hand but all he hit was the redstone face of the cliff Lone had positioned himself and Velda against. They, in contrast, remained cool and unrattled and their return fire was unerring. Two bullets pounded simultaneously into Seth, lifting him out of his saddle and hurling him to the ground in a lumpy, leaking heap.

It was over almost as quick as it started.

Coils of blue gunsmoke drifted silently down the slopes of the hill. For several beats the only sounds were the nervous stamping and blowing of the three horses now minus the riders they had arrived with.

Straightening from the half crouch she'd dropped into, Velda looked over at Lone and said casually, "Thanks for backing my play."

Lone's eyebrows lifted. "Didn't see where I had much choice. Once it was clear you were gonna draw gunfire it meant bullets would be flyin' my way too." He shrugged. "But it was bound to come to us pullin' triggers on those three. They were lookin' for trouble right from the get-go...I only wish we could've kept one of 'em alive long enough to say if it was true they were on the way to hook up again with Mitchum and where it was gonna be."

"The answer's got to be Pickaxe, just like we've been figuring," Velda said with conviction. "This bunch was made up of wanted varmints same as Mitchum. Their kind coming to this territory is almost guaranteed to mean one thing—they're aiming to pay a visit to Lobo's home away from home."

"So these three really are wanted by the law, eh?"

"For a fact."

As they talked, their hands, almost as if by their own volition, were busy ejecting spent shells and pressing fresh rounds into the cylinders of their Colts before re-holstering them.

"They're pretty low rung desperadoes from the Pine Ridge area," Velda continued. "I didn't recognize them right away because I'm not carrying any papers on them. But I finally remembered seeing their ugly mugs on postings back in Newbridge. Harley Reacher, Mort Nelson, Seth Robbins. Just before I left, there was a stage robbery outside of town and most folks were quick to believe it was their work. That would have upped the ante on them considerable."

"It also might explain Harley's remark about havin' some 'separate business' to take care before they caught up with Mitchum again," Lone mused.

"Could be."

Lone frowned. "If that was the case, wonder why Mitchum didn't stick around and do the stage job with 'em?"

"A fourth of the split from the take off that stage would have been peanuts to Mitchum," Velda replied. "I don't know how close you looked at that handbill on him that I showed you yesterday, but his latest, bloodiest crime was a train robbery down near Grand Island. His haul was estimated to be around twenty-five grand. But to get the job done he blew a section of the tracks and caused a passenger car to derail. A pair of nuns and a mother and her two children were killed in the wreck. So, Mitchum's haul was big, but so was the amount of heat it brought down on him and the increase in the reward on his murderous damn head."

Lone nodded. "Guess that makes it easy to see how he was runnin' too fast and hard to stop for any nickel and dime stage robbery when he needed to reach the safety of Pickaxe to escape all the bloodhounds on his tail."

"But what neither him nor Lobo Hines are figuring on," Velda said with frosty determination glinting in her eyes, "is that one of those bloodhounds—well, now two, with you siding me—isn't willing to stop at the Pickaxe city limits."

"Not willin'...or not smart enough?" Lone asked, grinning wryly.

"You tell me." Velda arched a shapely brow. "I'm going in for money and to bring down a vicious killer. You're going in to retrieve a stupid old horse."

"You bet I am," Lone agreed. Then: "Speakin' of horses, looks like I just gained three to choose from as a replacement for the grulla."

"They all look equally sound. That means you not only will have a mount you won't have to keep babying, but it also means," Velda pointed out, "you won't keep getting in trouble for riding Turk Mitchum's nag."

"Amen to that. Now, movin' on, what about these three gents who were kind enough to provide me all the new horseflesh to choose from?" Lone made a gesture indicating the sprawled bodies of Harley, Mort, and Seth. "I suppose you want to haul them into Lusk to claim the rewards on their heads?"

Velda surprised him by replying, "No. In the first place, I don't think they're in the Dead or Alive category. At least they weren't, not unless that stage robbery bumped them up. Either way, I don't figure they're worth the trouble. But even more than that, I don't want to take the chance of exposing myself this close to Pickaxe."

"Exposing yourself?"

"Yeah. It's something I should have thought of sooner." Velda scowled. "You see, about the time I was recognizing those three skunks, I also had the feeling Harley was beginning to recognize me in return. That's why I tossed out a phony name, to throw him off balance a bit. I don't mean he knew me by sight or anything but, let's face it, there aren't a lot of gals riding around packing a six-gun and knowing how to use it. I've been at this bounty hunting thing for a while now and I guess I've gained a sort of reputation."

Lone figured he saw what she was getting at. "So, if we took these bodies into Lusk, which ain't all that far from Pickaxe, it'd be advertisin' that the bounty hunter you is in the vicinity and it might queer your plan for passin' yourself off as a saloon floozy later on when you get to Pickaxe."

"You got it. Lobo Hines is careful about controlling the people who pass in and out of his town, but he's very open to any reports or even rumors finding their way in that might provide him an advance warning."

"Let me guess some more," Lone said sourly. "You're

wantin' to go to the trouble of buryin' these no-accounts, scatter their horses, and then make like what happened here never took place."

"It's the smartest and safest thing for what we've got left to do," Velda stated with conviction. "Furthermore, before continuing on to Lusk I guess I'd better swap my gunbelt and britches for a skirt and some face paint to try and be convincing for what I aim to pull off."

Lone grimaced. "Swell. I dig in the hot sun while you get gussied up."

"At some point my 'gussying up' is going to mean squeezing into a damn corset. Don't think that isn't toil on an equal scale," Velda told him.

CHAPTER SIX

SLOWED BY THE CONFRONTATION WITH HARLEY AND HIS bunch, it was late in the afternoon before Lone and Velda reached the town of Lusk. Spawned from a hay farming operation begun by one of the earliest settlers to the area, the resulting community became a small, tidy cluster of homes and businesses serving other farms and ranches in the area. Currently, it was experiencing a growth spurt due to an advancing spur of the Wyoming Central Railway. Evidence of this recent, sudden expanse, Lone and Velda saw as they rode in toward the older center of town, came in the forms of a couple new structures, a few more in the process of being built, and a handful of various-sized tents that they passed on the outer fringes.

In the heart of the more established business district they spotted what they were looking for standing three stories tall and boasting itself to be The Star Hotel. Smaller lettering running along the bottom border of the sign clarified its accommodations to include: Rooms – Restaurant – Bar – Barber & Baths.

"Looks like everything we need, all in one package," declared Velda as she and Lone reined up at the hitch rail out front. "You fry up a pretty good panful of vittles, McGantry, but I warned you about the swath I can cut through the menu of a full service restaurant. I'll be happy to demonstrate and even cover your tab if you care to join me—but only *after* we get checked in and I have myself a soak in a nice hot bath."

"Sounds good all the way around," Lone allowed. "I could use a barber shave and a bath of my own. And I've never had any trouble chowin' down on grub I don't have to fix myself."

Velda gave him a sidelong look. "Well the meal offer still stands. And a bath probably wouldn't hurt. But is it a good idea to get too trimmed and shaved and slicked up? Won't be that much longer before we move on to Pickaxe and, if we're going to try and sell you as my hardcase escort once we get there, continuing to look sort of rough around the edges—to use Harley's words—and not like some fancified Mississippi riverboat gambler seems a better way to help make the sale."

Lone frowned, but at the same time he wasn't too stubborn not to recognize a valid point when he heard one. The idea he and Velda had come up with for getting him accepted by Lobo Hines and his Gun Wolves was to present Lone as a tough hombre Velda had hired to get her safely across rugged country to her destination of Pickaxe. It stood to reason that somebody from that mold wouldn't be expected to look very polished.

"All right," Lone conceded. "I'll forget about shavin' the whiskers and gettin' my hair trimmed. I'll even make a point to hold back on flashin' my boyishly charming smile. And, just for good measure, I'll try to find a dog or two to kick when I'm sure somebody is lookin'. How's that?"

"Aside from your idea of humor, I guess it will have to do," Velda replied. "On the other hand, if you can't hold back more attempts at wit, better to get rid of them here than try them on the Gun Wolves when we get to Pickaxe. I suggest you'll stay healthier that way."

They dismounted and tied off their animals.

In place of the grulla, Lone had opted for a deep-chested black formerly ridden by Seth Robbins. It handled well and felt solid and strong under him but was no Ironsides. Not by a mile.

For her part, Velda had begun her transformation by trading her former attire to a wine-colored riding skirt and a scoop-fronted lemon yellow blouse that kept slipping off one shoulder or the other. She'd also added some color to her lips—a wine blush to match the skirt—and pinned up her cascading mane of hair, topping it with a dainty, short-brimmed straw hat. Lone had not missed nor was surprised that, all the way through town, the head of every man they passed turned to gaze longingly after her. And he was damned if he could blame them.

Since dealing with the three outlaws had taken so much time that they recognized they wouldn't be reaching Lusk until late in the day, Lone and Velda had agreed they might as well go ahead and spend a comfortable night there, then head out fresh for Pickaxe in the morning. Toward that end, at the Star's front desk they arranged rooms for themselves, boarding for their horses at a nearby livery stable, and the baths they had discussed.

While Velda (who signed in using her "Roxie Drew" alias) paid an extra dollar to have a private tub set up in her room, Lone settled for a pail of fresh hot water added to one of half a dozen wooden tubs permanently placed in an open air, fenced-in back yard for use mostly by ranch hands and such when they came to town. He and Velda then parted ways and agreed to meet up again at six in the hotel dining room.

After laying out clean socks and long johns for when he got dressed again, Lone stripped down and lowered himself into one of the cut-down hogsheads in the back yard bathing area. The contents of the big cask were relatively clean and already warmed by the afternoon sun. It was promptly warmed more by the attendant, a gangly, red-haired young man, adding a pail of fresh, steaming water.

"Plenty more where that came from, mister," said the lad. "I got a whole batch bubblin' on the coals over yonder and this ain't no busy time. Just sing out if you want some."

"Thanks, I'll do that," Lone assured him as he reached for the bar of soap he'd laid out with his items of clean clothing.

"For a quarter, I'll take your clothes and give 'em a good brushing while you get washed," the attendant further offered.

"You got a deal. Take your time, I plan on layin' back and soakin' here for a spell."

Which is exactly what Lone proceeded to do. Grateful he had the bathing area to himself, he took the chance to soak his mind in some quiet reflection while his body was soaking in warm, sudsy water.

Periods of reflection and introspection, sometimes quite lengthy, sometimes in brief spurts, were not uncommon for Lone. They made up much of the solitude he so cherished and often purposely created for himself. A recent example of the latter, in fact, had been a three week stretch he had undergone just prior to the encounter with Turk Mitchum—three weeks immersed deep in the forests and canyons of the Black Hills, well removed from any other person.

The reason for this had been to contemplate the immediately preceding series of events that had jarred and significantly changed the more stable life he'd begun to settle into. At the core of it was the gunning down of his partner and closest friend, a one-legged old mountain man named Peg O'Malley, shot and left for dead by a gang of marauders led by a specimen of human vermin called Scorch Bannon. Peg lived long enough to give Lone a slim clue about who had attacked him, but in addition to that he made a request to be returned for burial at a particular spot in his beloved Rocky Mountains.

Lone had fulfilled his friend's dying request, a task that came with some perilous twists along the way, before returning to pick up the cold trail of his killers. Lone also fulfilled that self-imposed task, the obligation to hunt down and make every mother's son of them pay in blood. Revenge or justice, Lone cared little for what anyone else might call it; he simply saw it as something he needed to do in order to feel somewhat whole again.

In the course of all this, others also died violently, some deserving, some innocent. Yet in the midst of the gunsmoke and bloodshed, Lone somehow became romantically involved with two very different women. One of them, a brassy saloon singer, had succumbed to a sudden illness. The other, a delicate Chinese orphan, had remained behind in Fort Collins, Colorado, promising to wait for Lone while he went off on the trail of the Bannon gang.

Thoughts of these two women—the tragically lost Maggie and the patiently waiting Tru—were at the heart of much of Lone's pondering during the time he spent in the Black Hills. There was, of course, nothing he could do as far as Maggie. But what of Tru? There was no doubt that strong emotions had developed between them. But was it enough, had they truly been sufficiently strong to last over the intervening time? Especially after the blood Lone had spilled, the lives he had taken in the interim? And now, just today, he'd had a part in cutting down three more. Did someone like him have the right to expect someone as soft and gentle as Tru to allow him into her life? Beyond the question of their opposing natures, it was hard for Lone to picture Tru returning with him to the horse ranch back in North Platte, the partnership he'd started with Peg, and even harder to see himself becoming part of her life in the Oriental community of Fort Collins.

By the time he rode out of the Black Hills, he'd reached at least one decision that should have been obvious all along: He owed it to Tru to return, as promised, so she could have a say in helping to determine if their path forward should be together or apart. He'd said his goodbyes, done all he could regarding Peg and Maggie, what remained was needing to reach a firmer close with Tru, not just leave things hanging fire.

Only now, yet again, something had cropped up that was diverting him from making it back to Fort Collins. It wasn't like he didn't still intend to go but, damn it, he had to go after Ironsides first. Tru would understand, wouldn't she? If not, that would for sure be a sign they didn't really belong together. And yes, there was the added complication of Velda. Not that she represented another romantic angle or anything but agreeing to partner with her in pursuit of Turk Mitchum meant a commitment by Lone that on top of retrieving Ironsides he also had to help Velda make it out of Pickaxe with not only her prisoner but with her hide intact.

"Jesus, how do I keep getting caught up in these things?" Lone groaned inwardly as he sat up in his cooling bath water. He cursed himself for letting what was supposed to be quiet reflection turn into this deeper pondering that threatened to ruin a soothing soak.

It was then that a sudden burst of jabbering voices tugged his attention away from his pondering and toward the voices.

CHAPTER SEVEN

"DOGGONE IT, JEROME, GET IN THERE AN START GETTING things ready. And be quick about it!" demanded a voice Lone recognized as the gent from the front desk who had checked in him and Velda.

The voice of the red-haired attendant wailed in response, "But I don't know nothing about attending no women, Uncle Walt. Aunt Hazel always takes care of female guests who choose out here."

"Your aunt is across town, helping Hester Wiggins birth another child."

"You'd think after six kids already, the Wiggins woman ought to have it figured out for herself!"

"Maybe so, but that don't appear to be the case." The arguing pair came into view, emerging from the rear door of the hotel. Where the lad Jerome was tall and lanky, his uncle was short and wide. The only bloodline resemblance seemed to be Jerome's thatch of carrot-colored hair and the reddish fringe above the ears of Uncle Walt's otherwise bald dome. "Now lay out some clean towels and pour some hot water in this corner tub," he continued ordering to the lad. "Once you've done that, pull the privacy screen over so Miss Hightower will feel comfortable and secure. Taking care of a woman isn't that much different from attending any other bather, as long as you keep this side of the screen."

The expression on Jerome's face said he was far from convinced. "What if she wants something more after I do the towels and water?"

"Then you reach through a seam in the screen and hand it to her. How hard is that to figure out?" Uncle Walt's tone was growing increasingly impatient. "Now hop to it, boy. Her father will be bathing on this side and he'll need some attention too. They'll be coming in any minute."

As Jerome trudged reluctantly across the yard toward where a rack of clean towels and a cauldron of bubbling water were situated against the back wall of the fence, his uncle turned abruptly toward Lone and said, "Please pardon this brief intrusion, Mr. McGantry. Most of our female guests prefer bathing in the privacy of their rooms like your friend Miss Drew, but we try to be accommodating to all."

"You ain't botherin' me none," Lone told him.

Uncle Walt smiled and for some reason saw fit to explain further. "In this case it's a traveling preacher and his daughter. They're living out of a wagon and can't afford a room. But I have enough Christian charity in me to at least provide them a place to thoroughly wash up coming off the dusty trail. After all, cleanliness is next to Godliness, as they say."

"Maybe," suggested Lone, "you could have extended your charity to also providing them a room for a good night's rest."

The hotel proprietor's smile stayed in place though pulled notably tighter at the corners. "I considered that, I truly did. But there's another saying about charity beginning at home. The hard fact is that I wouldn't stay in business very long and be able to provide for me and mine if I tried running the Star off a collection plate instead of out of a cash register."

"Yeah. Hard facts," Lone said wryly.

Further discussion between the two was cut short by Uncle Walt stepping away to help his nephew set up a privacy screen in front of a somewhat segregated tub that sat just to one side of the main building's rear door. The screen was in three hinged sections that opened to a length of about eight feet and stood six feet high on metal posts anchored by flat discs. No sooner was it in place than the building door opened and Lone caught a quick glimpse of a blonde-haired young woman emerging and stepping behind the barrier.

"Everything you need is right there, miss," Uncle Walt assured her as he promptly shifted the end of the screen so that it was tight against the outer wall, thus blocking anyone passing in or out of the door from seeing behind it. "There's plenty of clean towels and fresh, hot water just added to the tub. You want anything else just holler."

"Thank you. Everything looks fine," replied a soft voice.

A moment later, a new figure came out of the doorway. It was a tall, angular man, fiftyish, clad in a charcoal gray frock coat, matching shirt and trousers, the latter stuffed into high black boots. His face was weathered and set with an appropriately stern expression befitting a preacher. Thick white sideburns ran down the sides of his face from under the wide brim of a flat-crowned black hat. For a moment the sideburns made Lone think of Harley Reacher, but the ones displayed by the preacher were much more neatly trimmed and shaped.

"Pick any empty tub you like, Reverend Hightower," Uncle Walt said with a sweep of his arm. "Jerome will promptly fetch you clean towels and a pail of hot water."

"You are too generous, Brother Prescott," Hightower responded in a rich, solemn tone. "Be assured you will be mentioned in our prayers."

"Aw, think nothing of it. Least I could do. After all—cleanliness is next to Godliness. Right?"

Lone chuckled to himself. Uncle Walt obviously liked to stick with a good line when one occurred to him.

Something that then occurred to Lone, as he glanced up at how low the late afternoon sun had dropped in the cloudless sky, was that he ought to be ending his soak. He wanted to have enough time to make a pass around town before meeting Velda for supper. They'd convinced themselves that Turk Mitchum was likely all the way to Pickaxe by now. But there was always the chance for things to not be how a body suspected, even if it was only a slim chance. With that in mind, Lone figured it was worth putting in the effort to take a look around and make sure there was no sign of Mitchum—or Ironsides—in case the fugitive had perhaps found cause to tarry here for some reason.

He was out of his tub, dried off, and climbing into his clean longjohns, when the rear door of the hotel flew open once again and the two cowboys came barging out into the yard. It took about half a second to see they were drunk as skunks, the way they lurched and bumped against one another as they came forward. Both were young, not much more than twenty, clad in dusty, well-worn range clothes and scuffed boots. Each had a shooting iron strapped to his hip and a half-empty bottle of hooch gripped in one hand. One of them had a headful of curly black hair, his hat dangling down over his shoulders from a loosened chin string; the other wore a battered sugarloaf sombrero.

"Whooeee! It ain't even Saturday night but I have me a powerful hankerin' for a bath!" Curly Hair declared loudly.

"'Bout doggone time—you've needed one ever since I've knowed you," crowed his pal in the sombrero. And then both of them howled with raucous laughter.

Jerome, on his way back to the cauldron of hot water after pouring a pail of its contents for the preacher, stopped in his tracks and looked around. His expression was instantly clouded by anxiety. Moving with jerky reluctance, he turned all the way around to face the newcomers and said somewhat haltingly, "Does my uncle know you fellas came on back here?"

"Your *uncle*?" echoed Curly Hair. "Holy shit, you mean you're related to the owner of this fire trap yet the best job you can milk out of him is to slop water for a bunch of bare-assed strangers?"

"Here now," protested Reverend Hightower, who

was undressed to the point of having shed his coat and shoes and shrugged down his suspenders. "Your drunken boisterousness is not welcome here, and especially if you cannot display a proper amount of civility and respect!"

Curly Hair's jaw dropped and he rolled his eyes over to his partner. Then, his mouth stretching into a wide smirk, he said, "We sure enough don't got no civility or respect... But what the hell was that word 'boisterouserness' or whatever in blazes he said? I didn't know we even were able to do that."

"Who cares?" responded Sombrero. "We heard enough bluster out of this Holy Joe old bastard out on the street when all we was tryin' to do was say howdy to that little blonde filly he had with him. Hearin' some more out of his pie hole ain't our aim in comin' back here. When we saw where that blonde was headed, we came to offer our back scrubbin' services, remember?"

"A-course I remember. Where do you think that powerful hankerin' for a bath came from?"

The pair howled with another round of coarse laughter and then hoisted their bottles high for long, gurgling gulps.

When the bottles were lowered, Jerome took a tentative step toward the two cowboys. He was trying his best to form a stern expression on his young face as he said, "I think you fellas better leave now. You're welcome to come back after you've sobered up some."

The stony looks this got from Curly Hair and Sombrero were almost like lessons on *how* to look stern and menacing.

"You know what *I* think?" replied Curly Hair though clenched teeth. "I'm pretty damn positive I don't give a shit what *you* think... And if you pop off your mouth and try tellin' me and my pard any more what do, we're gonna stick that carrot head of yours down in one of these tubs and hold it there 'til the bubbles stop rollin' up!"

"No...I don't think I'd care much for that."

CHAPTER EIGHT

Lone had stood by, trying not to pay attention, telling himself none of it was any of his business and he ought to stay out of it. But it wouldn't work. The glint in Curly Hair's narrowed eyes was too mean, too piercing the way his glare knifed into Jerome. He wasn't going to let it go and the kid would be in way over his head. Curly had whiskey fueling aggression and stupidity in him and the obvious fear being emitted by Jerome was like a red flag beckoning his bullying nature all the more. Plus Curly knew he had an audience that he felt a craving to put on a show for—his partner naturally, and also Lone and the preacher, neither of whom he read as being willing to try and stop him.

Until the frosty tone in Lone's words indicated otherwise.

Curly's head swiveled around slow and his glare locked on Lone. "What did you say?"

"You heard me plain enough," Lone responded flatly. "Lay off the boy. Clear out like he told you. You and your pal go somewhere and crawl the rest of the way into your bottles, it'll be a lot safer for you."

"Safer how? From what?" sneered Sombrero.

"Yeah—safer from what?" echoed Curly. "From this punk kid? From the bony old preacher? Or maybe from you, standin' there in your bare feet and baggy-assed underwear?"

It was true that Lone hadn't had the chance to get dressed any farther than a couple buttons fastened up the front of his longjohns. But he refused to let these two rannies think that had him rattled any. "You figure you drunken pups got the bulge on me just because I ain't pulled my boots on yet?" he scoffed. "Hell, I've stomped rattlesnakes a lot more worrisome than the pair of you—in my bare feet."

The frostiness still in Lone's tone and also in his eyes gave Curly a moment's hesitation. But the whiskey in him and a sarcastic grunt from Sombrero standing beside him was enough to push past it, not let caution or better sense figure in.

"There's just one problem with that, snake stomper," he snarled. "You see, even the biggest, meanest rattler only has two fangs. But the thing you seem to be overlookin' is that my partner and me, between us, have got an even dozen. And if that ain't clear enough, I'm talkin' about the kind" —as Curly said this, his free hand dropped down to brush the holstered shooting iron on his hip— "that bites with lead."

"And you not only ain't got no boots on, you bigmouthed meddler," added Sombrero, "you also ain't got no leather strapped around your middle."

Naturally Lone didn't have his gunbelt buckled on yet, not over his underwear. It was where he'd laid it on a shelf attached to the side of the tub for the placement of discarded clothing and such. He'd positioned it there in a way purposely meant for his Colt to still be within quick, easy reach—except for the fact he now realized Jerome had buried it under the pile of clothes he had returned freshly brushed and folded.

Before Lone could make any response as far as the predicament this put him in, Reverend Hightower protested to Curly in a booming voice, "This is outrageous! You'd shoot a man over something as trifling as—"

His words were cut short by Curly suddenly drawing his pistol and triggering a round that blew the empty water pail out of Jerome's hand and sent it clattering across the ground. "Does that answer your question?" he demanded with a wild gleam in his eye. "You damn right I'd just as quick and easy shoot anybody who tried crowdin' me too far!"

The display made for a jarring, startling moment. But it also made a diversion that drew the attention of the two rowdies away from Lone for a moment. That gave him enough time to act, though not enough to try digging out his gun.

Instead the former scout bent slightly at the knees and reached down to grab the small wooden stool placed beside his tub to aid bathers getting in and out. Seizing one of its stubby legs, he scooped up the stool and hurled it as hard as he could in an underhand pitching motion aimed straight at Curly. The wobbly missile sailed the short distance and hit Curly in his gun arm, striking just behind the wrist with a sharp, cracking thud. The target yelped in pain and the gun went flying from his hand.

Following through on the momentum of his pitching motion, Lone lunged forward and veered to cover the distance between him and Sombrero in a single long stride. Reaching the man just as he started to claw for his own gun, Lone slammed into him with his left shoulder and drove him back against the nearest tub. The rim of the hogshead gouged into the small of Sombrero's back just above his gunbelt and the force of Lone ramming against him bent him in a way his body wasn't meant to go. He too yelped in pain but Lone cut it short by hammering his right forearm down on the man's throat and chin. As fast and hard as he could, he pounded two more such blows down on Sombrero, knocking off the big hat and releasing a spill of long, greasy hair to trail down into the water.

Straightening up, Lone grabbed a double handful of Sombrero's shirt and hauled him upright as well. Then, pivoting on his heels, he swung Sombrero halfway around, slinging an arc of water from his drenched tendrils of hair, before releasing him to go staggering against Curly who remained hunched over, clutching his injured arm and cursing. When Sombrero collided with his partner the two of them went staggering together in a frantic, stumbling entanglement until they toppled to the ground.

Lone closed on them immediately, pausing only to lean over and snatch up Curly's dropped gun. When the pair of troublemakers pushed free from one another and looked up, they found themselves staring into the gaping muzzle of the .44 from a distance of mere inches.

"Just hold still. Quit your squirmin' or I'll stop it permanent-like," Lone warned through clenched teeth.

The pair froze, exactly as ordered.

"Now you" —addressing a bloody-mouthed Sombrero— "reach over with your left hand real, real slow and lift that hogleg out of its holster then toss it away."

As Sombrero was complying, a harried-looking Uncle Walt came rushing out into the bath area carrying a rectangular tin can in one hand and a long-barreled Walker Colt in the other. "What the hell's going on?" he wailed. "Who fired that gunshot I heard?"

Jerome was quick to answer, saying, "It's okay, Uncle. Everything's under control now—thanks to Mr. McGantry."

The proprietor's eyes cut to Lone, scowling at the gun in his hand. "Was it you who did the shooting?"

"This was the gun, but I ain't the one who triggered it," Lone told him.

Now Walt's scowl dropped to the pair on the ground. "Where did they come from?"

"They barged back here with trouble in mind right from the start," said Jerome. "Didn't you see them come through the front?"

"No. It must have been while I was in the back room getting this can of coal oil to refill our lanterns. When I heard the shot, I - I grabbed this gun from the desk and—"

"Comes to that gun," Lone interrupted, "maybe you ought to go ahead and lower it, so it don't go off accidental the way you're wavin' it around sort of nervous-like."

"Yes. Yes, I guess I should," Walt agreed, dropping his arm and letting the big Walker hang at his side.

At that moment, a young woman's pretty face framed by blonde curls poked out through a seam in the privacy screen and asked in a faintly trembling voice, "Is everything okay out there now? Are you all right, Father?"

"Yes, daughter, I'm fine," answered Reverend Hightower. "Everyone is. Go on about finishing your bath."

"The hell everybody's fine!" Curly raised his head to protest. "My wrist is busted! I need a doc—"

Lone cut him short with a tap on the head from the barrel of his own gun. "Shut up, or I'll bust something else to match the wrist. Lay there and keep quiet, the both of you, until I say otherwise."

In a matter of minutes a town deputy, responding to reports of the gunshot coming from the hotel, showed up to take charge of the situation. He was young but cool and efficient and he recognized the two cowboys—whose names turned out to be Cletus (Curly) and Buster (Sombrero)—from previous incidents when they'd come in off the ranch and let too much liquor get them in trouble. The deputy took quick statements from Jerome, Hightower, and Lone, then led the two troublemakers off for a stay in the drunk tank (and presumably some doctoring, if necessary, for Cletus).

As soon as the deputy had taken away his new jail guests and things had settled down at the bathing area, Lone finished dressing and made his own departure. He still had time to make his planned pass around town, looking for any sign of Mitchum or Ironsides before joining Velda for supper.

The stroll through Lusk didn't turn up anything, but the supper meal made up for it. Everything very satisfactory. Steak with all the trimmings, fresh-baked cherry pie for dessert, pleasant company. And Velda lived up to her boast about cutting a memorable swath through any restaurant's menu, right down to a second piece of pie.

She also found time to remark on Lone's afternoon adventure in the bathing yard, saying, "I guess I owe that beat-up old grulla of Mitchum's an apology. I blamed him for repeatedly getting you in trouble. Turns out you're quite capable of finding some all on your own."

Wryly, and somewhat wearily, Lone could only reply, "Lady, you don't know the half of it."

CHAPTER NINE

Taking time to enjoy a full night's sleep on comfortable beds and eat another hearty meal for breakfast, Lone and Velda didn't get a particularly early start the next morning. The sun, only a bright smear in an overcast gray sky, was well above the horizon at their backs by the time they were on the trail headed west toward Pickaxe. Velda reckoned they still ought to make it by nightfall.

"Might work to our advantage, allow us to be less noticeable arriving under cover of dark," she mused.

"Or," Lone countered, "it might draw more scrutiny and an added dose of suspicion, like maybe we've got something to hide."

"Let them suspect all they want, as long as they give us a chance and think all they have to do is keep a close eye on us," said Velda. "When we're ready to make our move, we'll be happy to show 'em what they had a right to be worried about all along."

Once again Lone admired her bold determination. But, at the same time, he felt a faint twinge of concern thinking about the fine line between boldness and recklessness—a line that made a tightrope he himself sometimes had trouble staying balanced on. It looked like both of them might have to fight to maintain that balance in order not to let recklessness pull them into greater risk than they were already setting themselves up for.

As they rode, the morning remained overcast and chill. Frequent gusts of a damp wind made the chill bite even deeper.

Pushing a long tendril of wind-blown hair away from her face and shoving it down behind her upturned collar, Velda lamented, "This is sure a lousy trade for yesterday's sunny sky or last night's warm bed."

"No argument on that. Let's just hope the storm that appears to be buildin' in that nasty-lookin' cloud bank to the north"—Lone pointed with the jab of a finger—"don't roll down this way and make it even lousier."

This gave them cause to keep an eye peeled to the north as they rode on. As if this attention was some kind of jinx, the wind gusts began shifting to come more and more from that direction and the chances of the storm eventually descending on them seemed to increase accordingly.

Before that happened, however, something more immediate drew their focus. At first it looked like a dome-shaped tent erected up ahead in the rolling prairie grass. But then, as they got closer, they saw it was the canopy of a covered wagon halted down in the shallow depression of a dry wash. Riding closer still, it became evident why the wagon was halted there—its left rear wheel had fallen off the axle and the precariously tilted rig was stuck. A tall, lanky man in shirt-sleeves was straining to pry the axle up with a length of tree limb while a slim blonde woman stood ready with the wheel to try and push it back on if the hub rose high enough.

It took Lone a minute before he recognized the pair. It was the preacher, Reverend Hightower, and his daughter from yesterday's incident in the hotel bathing yard. In case there was any doubt, the large black lettering painted on both sides of the canopy—proclaiming SALVATION! IN ACCORDANCE TO THE WORD OF THE LORD—pretty much settled it.

The rushes of gusting wind and the intensity of the pair's struggle kept them from hearing the approach of Lone and Velda. Until, from the rim of the wash, Lone called down. "Looks like you could use a hand there, Reverend."

Hightower stopped straining on the tree limb lever and looked around in surprise. Despite the biting wind, his face was flushed and sweat-beaded from his efforts. After a moment, as recognition set in, his habitually stern expression was touched by a rare smile. "By all the saints!" he exclaimed. "Is that you McGantry—come to our rescue once again?"

Lone cocked an eyebrow. "I don't know about saints part, Reverend. But yeah, it's me. And I reckon I might be able to help some."

Hightower turned to the young woman. She appeared to be not much past twenty, slender yet shapely in a simple flower-pattered dress with a long skirt now billowing in the wind. A pale blue bonnet was tied around her pretty face with the blonde ringlets Lone had caught a glimpse of yesterday peeking out from under it. Her father said to her, "You remember

Mr. McGantry from that trouble at the hotel yesterday, don't you, dear?"

"Actually, we never really met," replied he girl. "But I recognize his voice, and I certainly recall hearing how he dealt with those dreadful men."

"Indeed he did," declared Hightower. "Mr. McGantry, allow me to formally introduce my daughter Hope. And let me once again—on behalf of both of us—express all gratitude for your timely intervention when it was sorely needed."

Lone pinched his hat to Hope, saying, "Pleased to meet you." Then, extending a hand to indicate Velda, he said, "Let me, in turn, introduce the two of you to my travelin' companion, Miss...er, Roxie Drew."

Once Velda and the Hightowers had acknowledged one another, Lone promptly stated, "Now, with that taken care of, I think we'd better jump pronto to the task of slappin' that wheel back on, Reverend."

"I appreciate your willingness and eagerness, but—"

"No 'buts' about it," Lone cut him short. "I'm not sayin' that to be pushy or rude. The thing is, I think you might have more to worry about than just gettin' your wagon fixed. You see that storm rollin' down from the north, don't you?"

"Of course. But I believe we have some time before it gets this far."

"Uh-huh. It may take a swing and not even get here at all. But the way it looks, it's rippin' pretty good up where it's at now." As if to emphasize Lone's words, an ominous distant growl issued from the wall of dense black off to the north. "That means," the former scout continued, "dependin' how far the gully your standin' in winds in that direction, there could be some heavy rain already pourin' into it."

Full understanding still didn't seem to register on Hightower's face.

So Velda helped it sink in, saying, "In other words, there could be a flash flood building up there that will mighty sudden turn this dry wash into anything but dry."

"My Heavens!" exclaimed Hope.

"It comes, there won't nothing Heavenly about it," Lone told her.

"Such a thing never occurred to me," muttered Hightower, looking distraught. "But if the possibility exists, then you are of course right—we must make all haste to get out of here."

"Trouble is, I don't think we'll ever get the wagon lifted high enough with that limb you're tryin' to use. It's too small," said Lone. "Hand me that axe I see strapped to the side of your wagon, I'll take it up the wash a ways and chop us something longer and sturdier. In the meantime, I suggest you ought to unhook your horse team and hobble 'em up on higher ground on the other side. In case a flood comes before we get the wagon fixed, you don't want to lose them still in their traces. We can always rope 'em back on quick to pull the wagon out once we get the wheel in place. You also—again, just in case—might want to take some of your most valuable stuff out of the wagon to high ground."

Hightower frowned deeply. "But our most valuable cargo is..."

He let his words trail off abruptly and then, after a somewhat awkward pause, Hope finished for him: "Bibles. We're hauling boxes of Bibles. Dozens of them, more than a hundred...We hand them out at our sermons. To help spread the holy word."

Lone frowned. "I ain't sayin' Bibles ain't important. But I was thinkin' more like stuff to help you survive in case the wagon is lost. Up to you to decide what that is, what's most important to you. But somebody hand me that doggone axe while you're makin' up your mind, so I can go fetch a proper lever and give you your best chance to save the whole shebang."

INCLUDING the time required for Lone to cut and trim a length of young sapling and drag it back to provide a longer, sturdier prying lever, it took the better part of an hour before the wagon wheel was finally on its hub once again. All the while, the wind was increasing in strength and driving steadily rather than just in gusts, pelting those involved in the effort with dust and sand and stinging small pebbles swept from the floor of the wash. Adding to this was the frequent ground-trembling claps of thunder coming from the advancing storm.

But at the core of it all was getting the back-breaking weight of the wagon lifted high enough for the placement of the wheel. Lone, who took no small amount of pride in his physical strength, was strained nearly to his limit. Enough so that at one point, disregarding the company he was in the presence of, he hissed through gritted teeth, "Jesus Christ, are those Bibles you're haulin' carved on stone tablets?"

Finally, however, a furious combined heave by Lone and the reverend got the hub raised to where Velda and Hope had the clearance they needed to shove the wheel on. From there, not taking time to fully re-hitch the pulling team, Lone quickly long-roped them to the wagon tongue and in that fashion got the rig pulled up out of the gully. As luck (or Providence, as Hightower would attribute in a prayer he offered up a little later on) would have it, only a matter of minutes passed before the first bubbling edge of water began filling the wash. Right after that, a higher, more wildly tumbling, frothing muddy brown wall came rushing over where the wagon had been.

Lone and the others had only a few additional minutes to savor the accomplishment and catch their breaths ahead of the full storm arriving with brilliant pitchforks of lightning sizzling across the sky and slicing, wind-driven sheets of cold rain hammered down by rolling, relentless growls of thunder. The four of them clambered into the canopied wagon and huddled there, exhausted and wind-buffeted, but relatively warm and dry.

CHAPTER TEN

"Pickaxe... Are you sure you want to go there, Reverend? Do you know what kind of place it is?" Velda's questions were spoken with genuine concern in her voice.

Hightower regarded her solemnly, calmly before answering, "It is a town. A town with citizens whose lives will be enriched by the word of God that it is my charge to bring them."

"I'm afraid," Velda countered, "you may find the citizens of Pickaxe not very receptive to the good you're meaning to do. From all reports, it is a town unlike any other you've likely come across. It's a haven for outlaws and scoundrels of every stripe, the worst from every surrounding territory. The only enrichment they're looking for in their lives is the kind measured in dollars and cents and usually taken at the point of a gun."

"You paint a very bleak picture, Miss Drew," spoke up Hope. "And yes, we too have heard the stories about Pickaxe. But we have traveled to other so-called 'tough towns' and came away feeling confident that the message put forth in Father's sermons made a difference. Not in everyone perhaps, but in many."

"And if one's goal is to truly challenge the Devil and his work," added Hightower, "doesn't it only make sense to go to a place where his evil influence is strongly rooted?"

Velda looked over at Lone as if appealing for him to back up the point she was trying to make. Though Lone's way was to seldom try and sway the behavior of others, the weight of her gaze made him feel obliged to say at least something.

So, with a fatalistic shrug, he drawled, "Seems to me, Reverend, you full understand what you and your daughter are headed for, yet you're bound to go through with it regardless. I respect your faith and the courage of you conviction. At the same time, though, I gotta float my stick same as Velda in suggestin' it might be smarter for you to swing wide and leave Pickaxe to the Devil and the claim he's already got staked on it."

The storm was gone now. It had raged for nearly an hour and then, the way early summer storms often do, let up almost as quickly as it blew in. The leftover clouds in the afternoon sky overhead were breaking apart and larger and larger patches of clear blue were being exposed. The level of the flash flood water in the gully that had formerly been just a dry wash had dropped considerably and the flow carrying it was only a sluggish crawl.

Once the rain stopped, Lone and the others had quit the shelter of the wagon and were then faced with the work of properly securing the wheel and replacing the items that had been offloaded in case the wagon was lost. Luckily these items had been wrapped in a heavy tarp that proved to have done a pretty good job of protecting them from the downpour. When it came to the wheel, for the sake of hurriedly getting the wagon out of the gully ahead of the anticipated rush of water, it had only been shoved onto the hub without taking any time to fasten it in place. In another stroke of good fortune, it turned out that Hightower possessed the foresight to stock a supply of tools and repair parts that provided him and Lone what was needed to snug the wheel properly back on the axle hub.

While the men were finishing the wheel repair, the women built a small campfire over which they brewed a pot of coffee. To go with this, Hope produced several slices of corn bread wrapped in an oilcloth, and a jar of honey to spread on them. When the wheel work was done, everyone gathered around the campfire and enjoyed a late noon meal of honeyed corn bread washed down by fresh, hot coffee. The relaxed conversation that took place during this was when it came out that the destination of the reverend and his daughter was Pickaxe.

Continuing the discussion resulting from this, Hightower said in response to Lone, "My daughter and I truly appreciate your concern, as well as that of Miss Drew. But I'll repeat my belief that the word of God is most sorely needed where, as you point out, the Devil has staked a claim."

"The other thing we're trying to point out," Velda told him, "is that you could find spreading the word mighty hard to do if those who've cast their lot with Ol' Scratch decide to run you out of town or, worse yet, silence you with a bullet."

Hightower sighed. "In the face of that kind of threat,

I rely on my unshakable faith in the Lord to protect my daughter and me."

After that, there didn't seem to be much more to say on the matter.

Hope, however, had a question of her own. "May I ask how you two are so familiar with Pickaxe? Have you ever been there?"

"No. No, we haven't. But, as I indicated earlier, we've heard plenty about it," Velda answered. Then, after a bit of an awkward pause, she added, "And, I guess you deserve to know, we're on the way there ourselves."

This naturally brought surprised looks to the faces of the Hightowers.

"Don't think that automatically makes us outlaws, though," stated Lone. "In spite of what we may have painted, not *everybody* in the town is an owlhoot of some kind. Though that still don't mean it's a place for gentle folks like yourselves to try and fit in."

"Why *are* you going there then?" Hope asked pointedly.

Lone met her probing gaze with a level stare. "Even though I've never crossed over the line, you've already seen I come from the wilder side of things and pack my share of bark. Hombres like me have a way of gettin' by wherever we take a notion to light for a spell."

"What about Miss Drew?"

"Miss Drew can speak or herself," Velda was quick to interject. "The truth of the matter is that McGantry is going to Pickaxe because of me. I'm going there for a job and I hired him to safely escort me that far. The job I'm seeking will be in one of the saloons—not peddling my flesh, to be clear, but as a hostess and entertainer. That's the line of work I'm in and, regardless of its other reputation, word has it there's good money to made doing that sort of thing in Pickaxe. Like McGantry, I'm someone who knows how to get by wherever I light for a spell."

Hightower listened to this with no expression on his face. When Velda was done, he regarded her with a gentle smile and said, "You sound as if you feel the need to justify yourself, my dear. That's quite unnecessary. Neither my daughter nor I judge—that is in the hands of one far greater than us. You need only be true to yourself and to Him... However, since it sounds like we're all going to be spending some time in Pickaxe, I invite you—and Mr. McGantry too, of course—to honor Hope and me by attending one of my sermons."

It took Velda a minute before a corner of her mouth lifted in a ruefully crooked smile and she responded, "Okay, Reverend. I can't speak for McGantry, but if we all last long enough after reining up in the Devil's backyard...you got a deal. I'll show up at one of your sermons."

"Splendid," declared the reverend. "I'll look forward to it."

"How about Mr. McGantry? I didn't hear a commitment from him," Hope said somewhat impishly.

Lone cocked an eyebrow. "Okay. Like Velda said...if we all last long enough, I'll show up too."

"As far as lasting long enough, you're already partly responsible for that," pointed out Hope. "After all, if you hadn't twice intervened—once at the hotel and again here when we were in the path of the storm flood—we might not even have made it this far."

"No need to make more of it than it was," Lone scoffed gruffly. "I just happened to be—"

"No. No, my daughter makes a valid point," Hightower interrupted. "If not for your timely aid on those occasions, we may very well *not* have made it to this point." He smiled. "It occurs to me that the hand of Providence is sometimes revealed in unexpected guises."

"Aw, come on now. That's reachin' awful far to—"

The reverend cut him off again. "But why tempt it? It further occurs to me that, since we *are* all bound for Pickaxe, why not finish the trip together? Unless you and Miss Drew plan on racing the rest of the way in great haste, our wagon won't slow you that much. After being delayed by the storm and the broken wheel, none of us are going to make it yet today. I don't mean to impose any more than we already have, but..."

And so it was that Lone and Velda found themselves cornered into going the rest of the way to Pickaxe in the company of the Hightowers. As Velda put it, commenting wryly under her breath so only Lone could hear, "After all, we don't want to get in the way of you serving the hand of Providence."

CHAPTER ELEVEN

LONE WAS THE FIRST ONE TO RISE THE NEXT MORNING AND it was only a matter of minutes before he spotted the column of smoke dirtying the sky off to the northwest. His experiences as an army scout for so many years caused an instinctive twinge of alarm in him at the sight. But no, it wasn't Indian sign, at least not signal smoke; Lone was pretty sure there'd been no Indian trouble in this area for some time. But the size of the smoke column indicated trouble of some kind, and a significant amount.

He continued eyeing the smoke as he stirred the previous night's campfire back to life and hung a pot of already prepared coffee fixings over the flames to start brewing. Crawling out of her own bedroll, Velda promptly noted his far-off gaze and followed it until she also saw the smoke column. "What do you make of it?" she said.

"Trouble. For somebody," Lone replied.

"For us, you think?"

"Not necessarily. Not unless we make it so."

After joining with the Hightowers yesterday, they had traveled a handful of miles together before stopping to make night camp in a flat, grassy oval partially encircled by a curving line of low, jagged rocks. Supper had been simple fare of pan biscuits prepared by Lone, salt pork and stewed tomatoes provided by Hope. Conversation was somewhat limited both during and after the meal as all were exhausted by the day's activities. They'd turned in early, with expectations for reaching their destination by noon the next day.

Anticipating possible interference with that now, as she and Lone stood looking at the distant smoke, Velda said, "If we keep running into things that slow us down or pull us off course, we're never going to make it to Pickaxe."

Lone gave her a sidelong glance. "Who said anything about gettin' pulled off course?"

"Maybe nobody said it in words. But I can see that look in your eye. Wondering what's going on over there—maybe more trouble you can get mixed up in—is tugging at you, isn't it?"

"Ain't like I go lookin' for trouble," Lone objected, scowling. "But yeah, I'll admit to wonderin' what's goin' on over there. Like I said, it sure looks like *somebody* is in trouble. By the location, it's likely a small ranch or farm—maybe a family with kids."

"What about a family with children? Trouble, you say?" This was Reverend Hightower, approaching from the direction of the wagon, pulling his suspenders up over his bony shoulders as he strode forward.

Lone pointed with a tilt of his head. "That smoke off yonder. I was speculain' it might be from a small family ranch or farm."

"Lord! If that's the case," said the reverend, "then it could mean some unfortunates—perhaps even children, as you suggest—in need of help."

"That smoke is a ways off and it looks as if the fire causing it has been burning for a while," Velda pointed out. "By the time we got there, I don't know how much good we'd be able to do."

"If there are injuries, then perhaps a great deal," insisted Hightower. "In the wagon we even have some medicines and bandages. We should go and do whatever we can. In fact, Hope and I *are* going. You two can get there quicker on horseback, we'll follow as soon as I hitch up the team. Please, I urge you to go on ahead and check it out."

Velda rolled her eyes and then leveled a glare at Lone. "All right, Hand of Providence, let's go see what kind of trouble we can find for you to get into this time."

Lone and Velda pushed their mounts hard and reached the source of the smoke in short order. Topping the crest of a long, brushy slope, they checked their animals and paused for a moment to look down on the scene that lay below in a small, shallow basin occupied by—as Lone had guessed—a modest-sized farm. Or, more accurately, what was *left* of a farm.

The house was a collapsed pile of smoldering ruins with a few flames still licking up here and there. About thirty yards beyond, a small barn was still burning strongly. Its roof hadn't yet caved in totally but was only a fiery skeletal framework from under which most of the smoke was pouring. On the ground between the house and barn lay scattered a half dozen bodies. Two were human, the other four were short, lumpy animal carcasses. Standing in the midst of this carnage were two men with their heads hung low. Their hats were removed and held to their chests with one hand, the other hand of each held the reins of horses they appeared to have only recently dismounted from.

"I make it the two still standin' down there ain't no part of whoever did the damage," Lone speculated. "They look like they just showed up."

"I read it the same," Velda agreed. "But we'd still better be careful going down."

"Always the smartest thing."

"With that in mind..." Velda twisted at the waist and reached back into her saddlebags. Due to their hasty departure from camp she hadn't had time to pin up her hair or apply any face powder or paint, but was still clad in the long skirt and off-the-shoulder blouse in order to maintain her saloon entertainer guise for the sake of having presented that to the Hightowers as well as in preparation for arriving in Pickaxe. Against the briskness of the morning she'd donned a short-waisted jacket over the scant blouse and hurriedly shoved her hair up under her retrieved Stetson. Sticking with her Roxie Drew role in front of their traveling companions, however, had prevented buckling on her gunbelt which, given this new development, seemed to need correcting. As a compromise, Velda now withdrew said gunbelt from its temporary storage in her saddlebags, but only long enough to pull the Colt from its holster. The belt went back in the saddlebag, the Colt got slipped into a pocket of the jacket. "There," Velda announced, "now I'm ready to be careful."

Down into the basin they rode, their sense of urgency considerably diminished due it appearing they were too late to make much difference. As they approached, the two men standing by the strewn bodies remained very still, watching them warily.

As they drew closer, Lone could see that the pair consisted of one man aged forty or so and a second about half his age. Possibly father and son was the impression that jumped to mind. The man wore baggy bib overalls over what was once a light blue work shirt now faded to almost silver, sleeves rolled three quarters of the way up thick-wristed forearms baked nut brown by the sun. The lad had on equally faded denim trousers and a collarless homespun shirt, pea green in color, with the sleeves cut off above his elbows, revealing stringy arms also darkened by the sun. Wide-set pale blue eyes on the faces of each and matching thatches of unruly reddish brown hair further marked a kinship between them.

They had the mark of farmers stamped all over them. Further evidence of this, and something Lone had been quick to take note of, was that neither of the men were visibly armed; though the horse whose reins were being held by the man had a Henry repeating rifle in its saddle scabbard.

As Lone and Velda reined up before them, the eyes of the man turned abruptly cold and hard. "If you're here to carry out more of Lobo's hellishness," he said with his lips peeled back in open disgust, "I guess you can see you're a little late. Some of your Gun Wolf buddies have already earned their pay. Henry's prize hogs are wiped out...and him and Belle right along with 'em!" The man's voice broke a bit as he spoke those final words—broke, in Lone's judgment, with a mix of sadness and barely controlled rage.

Velda's expression turned solemn and she gave a slow shake of her head, speaking softly. "We can't deny knowing about Lobo Hines and his Gun Wolves, mister. But we're just arriving to this area, and certainly had nothing to do with whatever happened here."

The look on the man's face faltered. He blinked. "You...You're a woman!"

Under different circumstances the reaction might have been somewhat comical. But not now certainly. Not with bodies strewn just feet away—and especially not with one of them, Lone realized belatedly, being another woman, a stout figure misleadingly clad in trousers and a bulky sweater.

"We're with a small party that made camp last night a short ways to the southeast," Velda explained further. "When we woke this morning and saw the smoke over this way, we thought we should come and see what the cause was and if there was any way we could help...I – I'm sorry we're too late."

"But," Lone added, "the rest of our party will be along shortly. They're comin' in a wagon. It's a minister and his daughter. If you want, I'm sure the reverend will be willin' to say some words over the departed, maybe bring a little comfort to any kin or other mourners."

The man looked at him with a sudden, strange kind of emptiness in his eyes. "Time was, that might've been a good thing to hear, stranger. Maybe it still will be to some. But as for me...I've come to reckon that God or any comfort coming from Him has pretty much abandoned this whole territory."

CHAPTER TWELVE

BY THE TIME THE HIGHTOWERS ARRIVED, LONE AND Velda had gotten a number of additional details from the two men they'd found on the scene when they first got there. For starters, the man's name was Fred Walburn, his son was Lee. They and a Mrs. Walburn (referred to as Letty) lived on a neighboring farm some miles to the west. They, too, had spotted the smoke from the burning buildings when they first rose this morning and had come...too late...to investigate its source and see if there was anything they could do to help.

The slain couple were Henry and Belle Milestone. They had two daughters—Molly and Stella, ages nineteen and twenty-one, respectively—who were unaccounted for. Speculation from the Walburns on what might account for their absence turned out to be almost as disturbing as the fate of the parents.

"It's all on account of those blasted hogs," Walburn had declared with an angry thrust of his hand to indicate the four animal carcasses strewn around the bodies of the farmer and his wife. "I tried to tell Henry he was bucking Lobo too hard by bringing them in against the warnings he'd been given, but he was too dang stubborn to listen."

"He was warned against raising hogs? By Lobo Hines?" Velda asked.

"That's right. More than once."

"What's Lobo got against hogs?" Lone wanted to know.

"Who knows? He just don't like 'em, I guess." Walburn gave a derisive snort. "Ain't that rich? He's infested the whole town of Pickaxe with human swine and keeps 'em around twenty-four hours a day—but out here on farm and ranch land he don't want the real kind."

"I guess you can see that these four here," Lee spoke up, taking over some of the explaining, "are boars. They're some kind of special breed, I forget the name. They're supposed to produce real top quality stock, so Mr. Milestone had them shipped in special from Denver. Next he planned on bringing in some good, solid sows for them to mate with. His plan was to start a sort of pork ranch to compete with the beef raised elsewhere in these parts."

Lone said, "So was it the beef ranchers who were crowdin' Lobo to shut down Milestone's plan?"

"Nah, they had nothing to do with it." Walburn scowled. "The beef ranchers hereabouts are mostly small operations and got no love for Lobo, nor him for them. Matter of fact, he said as much when he first started objecting to what Henry had in mind. Said it was bad enough he had cows and cowshit—pardon the language, ma'am—dirtying up the countryside all around his town, he was da—er, *darned* if he'd put up with pig stink on top of that!"

"This seems like an awful extreme measure to take for discouraging Milestone's plans when they were barely off the ground," Velda remarked, frowning.

Walburn gave her a look. "I thought you said you knew about Lobo Hines and his Gun Wolves?"

"I said we'd heard of them. But those kinds of stories often get exaggerated."

"Well I'd say there's a good chance that wasn't the case for any bloody tales you heard about how Lobo runs things." Walburn's eyes dropped once more to the bodies of Henry and Belle Milestone and a fresh wave of sadness pulled at his features. "I gotta admit, though, I didn't expect the lowdown scum would go this far so quick. Not, like you said, when Henry had only just got in his boars. Sending some Gun Wolves to cut down the animals? Yeah, that wouldn't have surprised me hardly at all...But to gun down these poor souls in the bargain..."

Lone gave it a beat after the man's words trailed off, then said, "You mentioned something about the daughters bein' missing. You think they're layin' off hurt somewhere? Or maybe they fled for their lives when the attack came—possibly to go try and find help?"

When his father was slow to respond, Lee said, "Molly and Stella are both pretty scrappy. Hard to picture them running out when their folks were in danger, especially their ma. Unless, maybe, if they saw both were already dead. But if they went for help, our place is as close as any and they should have made it before this." The lad paused and now his face took on its own deeply troubled expression. "Bad as it is to think...we're figuring the Wolves most likely took 'em."

"*Took* them?" Velda echoed.

An immediate response was interrupted by the sight of the Hightowers' wagon appearing on the crest of the basin and beginning its descent down toward them. All heads turned to watch. The reverend was at the reins, snapping them sharply and pushing his team aggressively down the slope. The wagon rocked and rattled as it rolled down and, on the seat beside her father, Hope jerkily swayed from side to side with the motion.

As they drew nearer, Lone could see Hightower's piercing eyes darting busily over the scene in order to take it all in and try to comprehend what was being revealed to him. By now the flaming rafters of the barn roof had finally collapsed but the middle of the former structure was still a crackling, boiling mass of fire. As he regarded this and the rest, the reverend's thick black brows knitted increasingly tighter.

"These are the folks I told you about," Lone said to the Walburns. "Reverend Harlan Hightower and his daughter Hope. They're bound for Pickaxe where the reverend believes the word of the Lord is, as he puts it, most sorely needed."

Walburn scowled. "I already told you how I feel about the Almighty having long since abandoned Pickaxe and all around it. I gotta give this sky pilot credit for being a bearcat to his faith, though, if he knows the score on that place and has the gumption to wade in anyway. But I'll also say that in addition to going in with the word of the Lord he'd better have himself a strong shield of the Lord to stand behind when he starts slinging it."

"He and his daughter believe their faith in what they're 'slinging' *is* their shield," Velda said with a quiet earnestness that caught Lone somewhat by surprise.

The wagon rolled in, rumbling and creaking, and the reverend hauled back on the reins to bring the team to a halt. His face bunched even tighter with anguish as his eyes made one more up-close sweep and then came to rest on Lone and Velda. In a hushed voice, he said, "It is as if the mouth of Hell breathed on this place."

"You ain't far off," muttered Walburn.

Lone swept a hand to indicate the speaker and his son, telling the Hightowers, "This is Fred Walburn and his son Lee. They're neighbors from off to the west. Like us, they spotted the smoke when they woke this mornin' and came to see if they maybe could help. Unfortunately, also like us, they were too late to do any good."

"And the deceased?" Hightower asked, gazing down at the bodies of the slain man and woman.

"Their names were Milestone. This ranch is—or was, I guess I should say—theirs," Velda answered. Then, bitterness edging into her voice, she added, "From the sound of it, they were killed for owning the pigs you also see slaughtered."

Hope gasped. "Killed over pigs? Who would do such a dreadful thing?"

"If you and you pa continue on into that Devil's pit called Pickaxe, like I hear you're planning to do," Walburn responded, "you'll be able to see for yourselves. The name is Lobo Hines and he won't be hard to find."

"Can you be certain this is his work?" Hightower said, frowning.

Walburn met the question with a hard stare. "Just as certain as you are of the Gospel you preach. Oh, Lobo might not have ridden out here to get his hands dirty doing the actual deed himself, but he was damn well the one behind sending his Gun Wolves to take care of it."

Hope shrank back on her wagon seat. "Are you saying this kind of outrage is common? We head some of the stories about Pickaxe and this, this Lobo person, but..."

"We tried to warn you," Velda reminded her.

Hightower gave a firm shake of his head. "That doesn't matter. And whatever happened here changes nothing...except, of course, for the unfortunates who suffered directly." He rose, preparing to climb down from his perch. "But before more words are spent on anything else, we must tend to these grievously departed and prepare to properly consign them into the arms of God, and Jesus who sits at His right hand. Are there kin or any especially close friends in the area?"

"There are two daughters," Lone said. "We were just startin' to talk about them when you rolled up."

"Do they live in the vicinity?" Hightower asked as he gained the ground and reached up to assist his daughter down.

Velda said, "They lived *here*. But there doesn't seem to be any sign of them."

"How can that be? You don't suspect ..." The reverend's eyes went first to the smoldering ruins of the house and then cut sharply to the fiery wreckage that had once been a barn.

"Nobody's had a chance to look around yet. Could be they got caught in one of the building fires," Lone allowed. "Or maybe they were injured or wounded in the attack and ran off to hide somewhere...But what we were just startin' to hear about when you rolled up was a whole 'nother notion young Lee was fixin' to explain."

When all eyes swung to Lee, he was ready to continue where he'd been interrupted. "Like I was saying, there's a chance Molly and Stella are missing because they got taken. What I mean is, took by the same as who did the killing and burning here—Lobo Hines' Gun Wolves!"

"Taken where? For what purpose?" Hightower wanted to know.

"Hauled off to Pickaxe," grated Fred Walburn, taking over for his son. "For what purpose? To work in Lobo's saloons and gambling joints...Do I have to spell it out any plainer than that, Reverend?"

"You sound like that sort of thing has happened before," said Velda, her gaze turning icy.

"It has. More than once," Walburn replied, his tone taking on what sounded to Lone like the weight of sorrow and shame. "Over the past couple of years, a half dozen or so young gals from surrounding ranches and farms—always pretty ones, like Molly and Stella both are—have gone missing and then been seen later on in Pickaxe, in places like I said. In one or two cases, the girls went willingly, lured by false promises of fancy clothes and money to be made. The other times they just got took...But they all ended up the same."

"What about their families? Their fathers?" Lone ground out through clenched teeth. "Didn't nobody try to get 'em back out?"

Walburn looked at him with hollow eyes and said dully, "Sure. In the beginning a couple of men went to town to reclaim their daughters. All that accomplished was to turn their wives into widows as well as mothers without daughters. You've got to understand—the name Gun Wolves ain't just a colorful term slapped on like the eastern newspapers or those writers of bloody dime novels toss around. They're real. An army of professional shootists and killers who do Lobo's cold-blooded bidding without hesitation or remorse. A common man, a simple farmer or rancher going up against them... even a dozen such men...is like tall grass trying to stand against a razor sharp scythe."

"Such a dreadful picture," murmured Hightower.

"I know. All too well," Walburn replied in that same dull tone. "A handful of us out here on the fringe have been looking at it ever since Lobo and his first dozen cutthroats showed up. We're too weak and too scared to fight, too trapped to pull up stakes and try to start all over again somewhere else. If we'd banded together right there at the beginning...maybe. But now..."

"The longer you wait, the more ground down and trapped you're gonna be," Lone stated.

Walburn eyed him. "Maybe so, mister. I admitted it, feeling trapped and weak, didn't I? But I was already here when the situation got dumped on me. I didn't go looking for it. So, I heard why the preacher is headed for Pickaxe, but what's the story for you and your lady friend? Knowing what you claimed to know already and hearing what more you've heard here this morning, you still figure to go there too?"

Before Lone could respond, Velda spoke in an odd, cautionary tone. "McGantry..."

Lone looked around and then followed the line of her gaze to a rim of the basin due south. Four riders had appeared there. They were paused, just looking, rigid in their saddles. Then, abruptly, they simultaneously spurred their mounts hard and came barreling down the slope.

CHAPTER THIRTEEN

The riders kept coming at a full gallop. Standing on the edge of the smoke and slaughter, Lone watched their approach and liked less and less what he saw. All four men were heavily armed, holstered six-guns slapping prominently on their hips. One of them wore a brace of pistols; another had a cartridge-laden bandoleer slanted across his chest. Each had a repeating rifle positioned for easy reach in a saddle scabbard.

Lone's right hand dropped in a slow, easy motion, thumbing the keeper thong off the hammer of his own holstered .44. Then he set his stance, facing the approaching bunch full on, feet planted at shoulders' width. Out the corner of his mouth he said, "Walburn, you know these hombres? More neighbors?"

"Not hardly. If I ain't mistaken, the heavyset one riding in the middle is Burt Kelson."

"Yeah, that's him," Lee confirmed.

"He supposed to be somebody?" Velda wanted to know.

"You could say that. He's a prime Gun Wolf. Sort of the lieutenant of the pack, Lobo's right hand man."

The horsemen came off the base of the slope and advanced across the floor of the basin.

Lone said, "Reverend, Hope...step over close to the wagon and hold there. Walburn, you and your boy stand tight by your horses."

Without being instructed, Velda moved several feet wide of Lone and took her own shoulders' width stance. Her hand slipped into the jacket pocket where she'd earlier put her Colt.

About ten feet short of where Lone stood, the riders reined up sharply. The cloud of dust churned in their wake came rolling to catch up, first smothering the four themselves then tumbling over Lone and the others. When the haze cleared, the man identified as Burt Kelson heeled his mount a couple steps ahead of the other three.

Kelson was thick through the body, not fat really, with a barrel chest and boulder-like shoulders to offset his girth. His face was broad and fleshy, split by a wide mouth under a blunt nose that tilted slightly upward to reveal flared nostrils packed with tufts of black hair. His eyes were a fraction too close together and looked down on Lone with piercing coldness.

Without preamble, he said, "We heard talk there was some kind of ruckus hereabouts last night. Came to find out if there was any truth to it."

The other three riders, one to Kelson's right and two to his left, slouched indifferently in their saddles. Unlike the speaker, who was clean shaven and attired in a fresh, crisp blue shirt, leather vest, and striped trousers tucked into polished boots, these others were considerably more careless in their appearance. Whiskery, wrinkled shirts, smudged britches and scuffed boots. Only their guns looked well-oiled and well cared for. And, Lone was quick to note, all had their keeper thongs unhooked.

In response to Kelson's statement, Lone said, "Guess you can see the answer plain enough."

The lead Wolf cut a quick glance over at the bodies and then back to Lone. "Yeah, and a sad one it is. Man's inhumanity to man...Pure shame how that keeps croppin' up, ain't it?"

"Don't know if the word 'pure' fits in anywhere," Lone drawled. "But what you said about sad and inhuman sure does."

"And let's not forget 'evil' neither." Now Kelson swung his gaze to the Hightowers. "Ain't that right, preacher? Without evil, you and the word of the Lord, like it says splashed across your wagon cover, wouldn't have nothing to bend folks' ears about, would you?"

"It's certainly true that evil exists in the world," allowed Hightower. "But it can only flourish if the words and teachings that the Lord passed down from the Holy Father are turned away from."

One of the men to Kelson's left, the one with the bandoleer slung across his chest, a gangly, narrow-faced specimen with jagged, yellowed teeth that he displayed when he peeled back his lips to snicker, said, "Well if you're on your way to Pickaxe, you're gonna find plenty of flourishin' waitin' for you there."

Kelson shot the man a sidelong look and he clapped his mouth shut. Then, returning his attention to the reverend, he said, "How about it, holy man? *Are* you on your way to Pickaxe?"

"Indeed," replied Hightower. "My daughter and I have been called to spread salvation and hope all across this wild, untamed frontier. The reputed conditions to be found in Pickaxe beckon us more strongly and, we recognize, may well prove more challenging than any previous place we've been."

The rider to Kelson's right, a swarthy individual with a pencil mustache and heavy-lidded eyes, spread his lips in a wide grin that revealed rows of big, gleaming teeth flashing in sharp contrast to those of his gangly comrade down the line. "You and your *daughter*?" he blurted. "Whooee, you Holy Joes sure know how to turn out fine fillies. You bring that to town, I definitely might have to come around and look to get me some salvation!"

"Shut up, Lasko," barked Kelson. "That goes for the rest of you, too. Keep your yaps buttoned while I'm havin' my discussion with these folks."

Sour expressions formed on the faces of the other three men and they shifted a bit restlessly in their saddles, but none voiced any objection to the way they'd been spoken to.

Lone took the opportunity to address Kelson again, saying, "Speakin' of what we're discussin', you mentioned you came out here because you heard talk there'd been some kind of ruckus...Care to say where you got that kind of talk?"

Kelson eyed him. "I might, I might not. What's it to you anyway? You ain't even from these parts."

"Man comes on a thing like this," Lone told him, "he don't have to be from any particular place to have a gut reaction makin' him want to see something done about it."

"You sayin' *you* intend to do something about it?"

"Ain't so much a matter of intendin'," Lone replied. "But was I to somehow find the yellow curs who did this in my gunsights, it'd be mighty satisfyin' to send 'em through the gates of Hell ventilated by my bullet holes."

Kelson squinted. "You *are* new around here, ain't you? You know who I am?"

"Heard a name. Kelson. There more to it?"

"Damn right there is! The full of it is *Burt* Kelson. I work for Lobo Hines. And if you don't know about him, you'd better listen real tight and learn real good. Lobo runs everything in and around Pickaxe and he long ago laid down a set of rules that amount to the law over the whole works." Kelson paused, puffing out his chest. "*I* run the crew—which includes these fellas here with me now and plenty more in town—charged with enforcin' those rules. And one of the main ones, just so you get the message clear, is that any ventilatin' done on account of wrongdoing or whatever, gets taken care of only by us."

Velda couldn't hold back. "So does that mean you intend to be the ones to properly ventilate the vermin responsible for what took place here? If that's the case, then oughtn't you start hunting them down instead of worrying about somebody else doing the job ahead of you?"

Kelson cocked an eyebrow in her direction. "When and how we operate is our call to make, missy. We don't need no outsiders showin' up to horn in and try to tell us our business." The Wolf lieutenant paused, the sharpness of his arched brow easing some and a sly curl to his mouth replacing it. "On the other hand, there might be some hornin' in allowed for a pretty gal like you. Are you part of the Holy Joe show, too? If so, I might have to back up a step and throw in with what Lasko said about comin' around to get me some salvation."

"If there was any sincerity behind your talk of salvation, then you could start with cleaning up the crudeness with which you address young women," declared Hightower. "And speaking of young women, did the talk you heard concerning the trouble out this way mention anything about the daughters of this slain couple being unaccounted for?"

"I was hopin' it was the daughters maybe makin' it to town to try and get help that brought these hombres out," said Lone. "If not that, then how *did* word get to Pickaxe?"

"We don't know nothing about the Milestones' missin' daughters," Kelson was quick to respond. "And there's already been too much talk in the past about that kind of thing—frisky farm gals runnin' away from the hard work and drudgery of their lives and then the town endin' up blamed for lurin' 'em off. Nossir, we ain't goin' through that again so don't nobody try startin' it. If those girls are missin', then their bones are probably at the bottom of one of these burnt heaps."

"Then that still leaves the question of who was spreadin' word in town about trouble out this way when not even the Milestones' closest neighbor" —Lone made a gesture to indicate Fred and Lee Walburn—"knew anything until they woke this morning and saw the smoke from over here."

"Enough already!" Kelson barked. "I tried to make it clear that any question askin' or anything else concernin' trouble like this will get took care of by me and my rules enforcers. I'll cut you newcomers some slack on account of you didn't know how things run hereabouts. But you do now, so see to it you remember." He cut a hard gaze toward Fred Walburn. "But you damn well knew, Walburn. You should have told 'em the straight of things right off."

Walburn was quick to respond, saying in a stiff tone, "It might not be something somebody like you would understand, Kelson, but finding Henry and Belle gunned down and burnt out like this gave me concerns that seemed a lot more important than explaining to these strangers about the pecking order of things surrounding Lobo Hines."

"You gettin' mouthy with me, Walburn?"

"I'm telling you how it is, that's all."

Glaring at Kelson, the good reverend said, "In the name of decency, man, have some compassion for Mr. Walburn's grief and show some respect for the departed. You are bickering over the bodies of two of God's children lying slain amidst swine. They need to be cleansed and prepared for a proper burial, with friends and loved ones in attendance and words of devotion spoken to hasten their souls to Heaven." Hightower paused, his glare growing more intense before adding, "If you cannot show appropriate reverence for such proceedings, at least allow time and space for those who wish to. You should concern yourselves with fulfilling your roles as enforcers and hold to account whoever is responsible for this atrocity."

"You gonna let him talk to you like that, Burt?" wailed the man with the bandoleer across his chest. "What-all was that mouthful of stuff he gargled out, anyway?"

"Pay no never mind to his high-minded gobbledygook," Kelson growled. "These Holy Joes carry on like that so's the suckers don't have time to stop and think what a crock it is they're bein' asked to swallow. Ain't that different from a snake oil salesman, except sky pilots don't even provide anything you can pour out of a bottle...It's all promises and hot air nobody has to back up until somewhere in the Hereafter."

Hightower smiled a thin, faintly mocking smile. "If you continue feeling that way, there's no doubt the air in your Hereafter will indeed be very hot."

Kelson winced, momentarily taken aback. Then the look passed, and his mouth formed a grimace. "To hell with this. Let these weed planters go ahead and plant a couple of their own in peace. Maybe they'll want to dump in some dead pigs for fertilizer. Ha!" Kelson wheeled his mount halfway around then jerked hard on its reins to make it rare up on hind legs. Sweeping a flinty gaze over those standing in front of the dead and smoldering, he grated, "Go ahead and do you prayin' and plantin' out here where you think you amount to something. But any of you come on into town—that means any of you strangers or you either, Walburn—you'd damn well better walk tight according to Lobo's rules. 'Cause in Pickaxe, you don't amount to much more than a scatterin' of pesky pissants barely worth swattin'. See to it you remember!"

With that, he finished turning his horse and then spurred away as hard and fast as he'd ridden in. The other three fell in behind him and each drew a handgun with which he burned some powder firing shots into the sky.

CHAPTER FOURTEEN

"I TOLD YOU SHE'D GET 'EM THROUGH! I TOLD YOU HILARY could be counted on!" Melvin Dekker clapped his hands together with a loud pop and then ground the palms exuberantly. "That girl has the face of an angel but more steel in her spine than a Union Pacific spur track."

"All things considered, that's a hard claim to argue against," replied Leland "Lobo" Hines in a measured tone. "Though, not to be negative, you can understand how there were times when it was hard to keep my hopes up. It's been a long haul to here from that armory down in Kansas, with some damnably worrisome setbacks along the way."

"I'm the last one you need to remind about that," Dekker said, frowning under a momentary faraway look that passed through his eyes. "I was there when the raft overturned in that swollen river, remember? Swallowed enough muddy damn water to irrigate half of Arizona before we got those crates saved and dragged up on the bank. I was there again when that federal posse ambushed us in those twisty canyons north of Benkelman. Lucky for us, there was a couple more twists than those murderous hounds figured on and the bloody remains of us got out by the skin of our teeth."

"I know, Mel. Believe me, I know how much of a steely spine you showed, too, to keep those guns moving, even after most of your crew was shot to ribbons." Lobo's tone was earnest and soothing. "And, when everything was closing in and looking ready to fall completely apart, coming up with the idea to hide the rifles in the wagon of that traveling preacher where none of the snoopers would ever think to look—that was borderline genius!"

Dekker wagged his head. "There again, I gotta give a big part of the credit to Hilary. She was the one who spotted the close resemblance between herself and the preacher's daughter. From there, we worked out the rest of it together—snatching the girl in order in order to force the preacher to cooperate, then loading the guns in his wagon and Hilary taking over as the daughter so's to steer their course for arriving here while I came on ahead with his brat as insurance to keep the preacher in line if he ever wants to see her again."

"Yes, and over three weeks it's been since you set that desperately clever ruse in motion. Three weeks with nobody—not you, not me, nobody—knowing for sure what kind of progress Hilary and her holy man were making across some mighty rugged country." Lobo looked torn between a scowl and a sigh of relief. "Thank God that not-knowing business is over. I can't tell you how much I hate having something—especially something this big—hanging fire and me not being able to personally grab hold and finish making it happen."

"Well, the way it stands now you're only a whisker away from bein' able to grab hold and finish your deal, Boss," said the third man in the room. Burt Kelson emphasized his statement with a firm nod of his head. "Yessir, the Milestone farm—what's left of it, I reckon I should say—ain't but an hour's ride out of town. 'Bout double that, I suppose, for a wagon to roll in. Soon as it gets here, though, you'll have the big haul you been so anxious for."

This conversation was taking place in Lobo Hines' private suite on the second floor of the Gold Tip Hotel. The setting was well appointed, though not extravagantly so; the furnishings all solid and basic, dark woods and leather in abundance, a masculine tone clearly evidenced.

The man himself, Lobo Hines, was of average height and build. Trim, yet projecting a sense of coiled-spring strength and an overall aura of power. His eyes had a faintly Oriental cast, dark and quick under thick, straight slashes of coal black brows that stood out in contrast to a cap of short-cropped, gray-flecked hair. His facial features were ordinary, except for a wide, expressive mouth equally capable of stretching into an ingratiating grin or twisting cruelly.

His attire, much like the furnishings of his suite, was of top quality yet lacking any flamboyance. Tan trousers, crisp white shirt, tailored vest with black leather panels in front and a silky weave in back. The turquoise clasp of his string tie was the closest thing he came to any kind of showy display. And while he seldom openly wore a gunbelt, in a special holster sewn inside his vest was snuggled a nickel-plated .38 caliber Colt "Lightning" with a two-and-a-half-inch barrel.

In response to Kelson's assurance about the preacher's wagon being so close at hand, Lobo's forehead suddenly puckered above a pained expression. "It's the damnedest thing," he groaned. "Knowing that blasted wagon is so close yet I still can't get my hands on its cargo—that's almost worse misery than all the weeks of not knowing *where* the doggone thing was."

Kelson's own expression took on a look of concern. "You ain't sayin' I should have brung it back with me, are you?"

"No, no I didn't mean that." Lobo made a dismissive gesture with one hand. "We worked too hard to keep a lid on this whole undertaking to get overanxious and careless now. You did the right thing, leaving the wagon to come in on its own."

Kelson looked relieved. "Good. That's what I figured. It sure was a surprise to find it there, though, when I took some boys back out early to have a daylight look at how we left things last night. Been just the wagon I might have thought different. But with that neighbor Walburn on hand, plus those two other strangers...well, I put on an act about comin' to check after hearin' reports of a ruckus and left it at that."

"They seem to buy that okay?"

"Walburn was givin' me the stink eye, I expect he had his suspicions. But he knew to keep his mouth shut, at least in front of me." Kelson frowned. "As much as anything, the lot of 'em seemed het up about the missin' daughters."

"Yes, I suppose that hue and cry will start up again." Lobo balled his right fist and pressed it into his left palm. "That pig-headed damn Milestone, standing up to me the way he tried to do left no choice but to take harsh action taken against him. Give one of those scrounging farmers or ranchers an inch, they'll read it as a weakness they can take more and more advantage of. Death and destruction is a hard line that sets them straight, wipes out notions of resistance. But taking their young gals like we've done a few times, that stirs something different, something deeper and somehow more bitter...I almost wish you would have gunned them Milestone girls along with their parents and the pigs, maybe left them to the fire."

"I came close to makin' that call, Boss," Kelson claimed. "But I hadn't seen those sisters in quite a spell and, wow, they've got awful pretty and well filled out in the meantime. It seemed a plumb shame to cut 'em down and let all they have to offer go to waste. Once Miss Sarina gets done showin' 'em the ropes, they'll bring a lot of pleasure to a lot of the fellas here in town."

"Yeah, I guess you're right. It's done now, nothing for it but to let it play out," Lobo allowed. Then, with a sly smile, he added, "And I'm also guessing you have plans to partake of some of that pleasure for yourself, am I wrong?"

"Well, now that you mention it..." Kelson let his words trail off and turn into a suggestive chuckle.

Dekker waited for the pair to finish their bawdy exchange and then said, "Getting back to the wagon and the guns—you say we can expect them here in a couple of hours, Burt?"

"No," Kelson disputed, "I said it'd take the wagon a couple hours to get here. The thing you got to remember, though, is that the preacher was makin' noises about givin' a proper send-off to the Milestones. If he plans on readin' over 'em, maybe hangin' around while

Walburn gathers some more neighbors and they go ahead with a burial...Well, that could take a while. Might even be toward evening before they roll in."

Scowling, Dekker exclaimed, "Hell! Now, with everything so close yet still seeming so far, I'm the one getting overanxious." He was a tall man, more than an inch over six feet, with broad shoulders and a flat stomach. His face was classically handsome, especially for someone pushing forty, complete with clear blue eyes and a widow's peak flowing back to thick brown hair showing no hint of gray. He wore a bronze-colored corduroy jacket over a gray shirt and pants. A black-handled Remington revolver in a tooled holster, also black in color, hung comfortably on his right hip.

"Take it easy, Mel," Lobo told him. "I know how you feel, but we need to be patient for just a little while longer. The gold Toneka knows the source of and is willing to part with to get his hands on those rifles is worth five times what we could get for them anywhere else. That's makes a bit more of a wait bearable, don't you think?"

"Yeah, yeah. I just hope that red devil ain't the next one who starts getting impatient."

"Everybody knows an Indian can be patient as a stone. Besides," Lobo grunted, "Toneka has no choice. Without the rifles, he's just another young hotblood with pent-up anger and no outlet for it. With the rifles he becomes an instant warrior chief who can lead a pack of other hotbloods like himself on a final, futile surge to spill as much more of the hated White Eyes' blood as they can before going down in a blaze of glory."

"As long as they don't take a notion to turn around and run that surge straight back at us," said Kelson.

Lobo gave a short laugh. "Toneka might be crazy but he ain't stupid. He knows that a pack of can't-shoot-for-shit braves, even armed with the latest model repeaters, ain't no match for our townful of experienced gunnies. No, I'm confident he'll go looking elsewhere to find his glory."

"Even if what you say about an Injun's patience is true," said Dekker, not looking fully convinced, "what if Toneka is so eager to cut loose he ain't waiting to be notified about the guns but is on the prowl looking on his own for them to show up? The preacher and those two strangers Kelson mentioned were attracted by the burning Milestone buildings—what if Toneka spotted the smoke too, and came for a look-see?"

"In the first place," Lobo said, an edge of impatience creeping into his voice, "Toneka's camp on the rez is miles away from the Milestone farm. Too far to spot any lousy smoke. Plus, he ain't on the prowl because he's staying put waiting for me to let him know when the guns get here. And even if he did spot the preacher's wagon, he wouldn't know to make anything of it. He has no clue that's how the rifles are coming in."

"Yeah, you're right," conceded Dekker. "I'm letting myself get worked up over nothing."

Lobo strode toward a liquor cabinet over against one wall and motioned the others to follow him. "Come on. It might be a little early in the day, but I think we could all use a stiff belt. Partly to celebrate, partly to settle ourselves down. This gun deal is going to be the biggest single money maker we've ever pulled off. It's foolish to let it tie us in knots, especially now that's it's so close to paying off."

"I'll drink to that," declared Kelson with a big grin.

Once some top quality brandy had been poured and each man had taken a pull, Lobo said, "A final thing I'm curious about, though, Burt. Those two strangers who were also there at the Milestone farm. What did you make of them?"

The Wolf lieutenant pooched his lips thoughtfully for a moment before replying, "I ain't altogether sure. They'd been travelin' in the company of the preacher and Hilary for a spell, but weren't really *with* 'em, if you get what I mean. It was just a case of 'em fallin' in together 'cause they were all headed for the same place. Here to Pickaxe.

"As far as the pair themselves, I'd say they each got a little bark on 'em. Nothing too worrisome, though, I don't think. I reckon the fella for a drifter, not so much a cow puncher but more like ex-army or buff hunter. Carried a side gun like he knows how to use it some, but not no regular gunny. The girl's a little harder to figure. Pretty, that's for sure. But no school marm and no gal lookin' to sell her favors, neither. Like I said, kinda hard to figure...But, like I also said, I don't see either of 'em as bein' particularly worrisome."

CHAPTER FIFTEEN

"This thing," said Velda, "is getting a lot bigger than just running down Turk Mitchum and retrieving your horse."

"Only if we let it. As far as how it concerns us, I mean," Lone replied.

"You said something similar when we first spotted the smoke. Yet here we are, smack in the middle of the tragedy that happened here, and what it all ties to."

"Ain't nothing we've seen or heard this morning," Lone said stubbornly, "that makes things any different from what you been tellin' me all along about Pickaxe and Lobo's Gun Wolves."

"Like hell," Velda hissed just as stubbornly. "This is far more vicious than the stories told to me and what I related to you. Pickaxe was presented as a haven for owlhoots and scoundrels to hide out and, yeah, sometimes for planning new raids at outlying locales. But never as such a scourge on decent folks trapped in the town or the surrounding countryside—a hell pit spawning rape and killing and demanding complete subservience else risk getting killed for something as petty as raising *pigs*, for God's sake! Not to mention having innocent girls spirited away in the middle of the night to spend the rest of their lives in unspeakable misery and the worst kind of servitude!"

Velda was worked into far more of a state than Lone would have expected from her. Not that he didn't share her revulsion for what had been done to the Milestones or for other acts they'd heard blamed on Lobo Hines and his Gun Wolves over the past few hours. But in his time, especially when scouting for the army during the years of Indian conflicts, Lone had seen acts of savagery —committed by both sides—that pretty much numbed him to outward reactions and taught him to control his rage. Until the time was right to release it in measured doses.

"At the very least," Velda continued in a strained voice, "when we get to Pickaxe we must try to find the Milestone sisters and free them."

"Okay. We'll do what we can," Lone told her, recognizing that now wasn't the time to try and point out the odds against pulling off such a rescue with the limited information they had and without making themselves prime targets for every gunny and cutthroat at Lobo's disposal. But what the hell; they were already well on the way to achieving that with their original reasons for going to Pickaxe. What difference did sharpening a couple more sticks to poke the bear with make?

It was past noon. Lone and Velda were leaning against the sloping trunk of a fallen tree in a sparse grove of ash and spruce about fifty yards removed from the remains of the Milestone house. Also within the grove, though somewhat apart from where Lone and Velda were quietly conversing, a handful of the slain couple's neighbors were gathered around two freshly dug graves. The bodies of Henry and Belle Milestone, wrapped snugly in clean linen supplied by Mrs. Walburn and a couple of the other wives who'd been notified and were now in attendance, lay on slightly charred wood planks salvaged from the torched barn and positioned beside the graves. It had been the consensus of those present that, in as much as Reverend Hightower was at hand and there was no known next of kin except for the missing daughters, a burial ought to go ahead and take place even without fully constructed caskets.

Lone and Velda had felt obliged to stick around, Lone even pitching in to do part of the digging. Now that everything was ready and as many mourners as could be reasonably expected to show up were assembled, it was time for the reverend to say some words. Lone and Velda pushed away from their tree trunk and moved to stand with the others. The men removed their hats, the women bowed their heads. In rich, soothing tones, Hightower read a pair of Bible passages, added some solemn yet comforting remarks of his own, and the service was complete.

Selected men stepped forward to man the lowering ropes that had been slipped into place under each wooden plank and, one by one, the bodies were eased down into their final resting places. Once the ropes were removed, Lee Walburn and another young man began silently shoveling from the mounds of displaced earth to cover over the deceased. Everyone else edged away from this activity and milled for a bit on the fringe of the grove, preparing to leave but most of them taking a moment to first thank Hightower for the impromptu service he'd conducted.

In the midst of this, the second young man who was helping Lee cover the graves suddenly threw down his shovel and exclaimed, "No! No, I can't let it go like this without saying my piece. Before all of you scurry away back home, back to your hidey-holes like the meek, frightened sheep you've all become, you're going to listen to me!"

The lad moved away from the graves and strode closer toward the partially dispersed gathering. He couldn't have been more than a year or two past twenty, tall and rawboned, with an even-featured, sun-bronzed face under a curly mass of brownish hair shot with pale streaks that also came from hours in the sun. Lone had noticed his arrival earlier, in the company of an older man and woman he reckoned to be the young man's parents. He heard them referred to as the Doyles, the son as Billy.

Right from the first Billy had appeared particularly distraught. He'd immediately pulled Lee Walburn aside and the two of them had talked quietly but animatedly for some time, Billy looking more and more anguished throughout. And then, while the bodies were being prepared and the graves dug, Billy had gone off by himself to several times circle close to the still smoldering heaps that had been the house and barn and to also roam out through the surrounding brush and tall grass. Searching, Lone guessed, for some sign of the missing daughters—something several others had already done without success.

During the graveside service by Reverend Hightower, Billy had stood between his parents, each of them with a hand on his shoulder as he hung his head and sobbed openly. By then Lone had concluded that the young fellow's grief and anguish was as much for one of the missing daughters—a sweetheart, it seemed obvious—as for those actually going into the ground.

And now the torment inside apparently needed a stronger release than just tears. "How much longer," Billy wailed, "are we going to go on like this? Living—if you want to call it that—under the bootheels of Lobo Hines and his rabid Gun Wolves. And, at their whim, maybe not even being allowed to do that much, to keep living."

His father, a burly man with iron gray sideburns and a weathered face clenched by its own anguished expression, took a step toward him, saying, "Son, I know how—"

"No. Don't say you know how I feel, Pa," Billy cut him off. "Because you don't. You don't *want* to know how I feel."

"I know you're sad and upset. I can understand that much, can't I?" pleaded the elder Boyle. "Everybody here liked Henry and Belle...and, and Stella. And Molly, too. A number of us tried to tell Henry not to push so hard with his stubborn idea about raising pigs yet—"

"What you mean," said Billy, interrupting again, "is that you tried to tell Henry not to do anything that would displease the great master Lobo Hines! Just bow down like all the rest of you. Do everything but lick

Lobo's boots for him—isn't that what it really amounted to?"

"How dare you talk to your father that way, you impudent pup!" growled one of the men standing nearby.

Billy spun on him. "Why? What are you going to do about, Mendenhall? You've already shown how gutless you are when they took your daughter last year and put her to work in Lobo's Lucky Nugget Saloon. You didn't say or do a damn thing, did you?"

Mendenhall scowled fiercely. "Sally ran off on her own. That's what she wanted, how was I supposed to stop her? They're treatin' her good, she likes it fine. She even sends money home to me and her ma sometimes."

"And so is everybody here supposed to pretend that's also what happened to Stella and Molly Milestone?" Billy's eyes blazed. "After Lobo's Gun Wolves shot their parents and burned down their home, they decided to run willingly off to Pickaxe where they too can be treated good and make money?"

"Try to take it easy, Bill," said an elderly gent with white whiskers and watery blue eyes. "We all know you and Stella had begun seein' one another of late and so this has got to hit you extra hard. But don't go gettin' too wild in your ideas, boy. Come tomorrow, after these coals have had a chance to cool all the way so we can proper dig through 'em, some of us will return here with you and—though this ain't pleasant to conjure neither—we'll likely find the remains of Molly and your Stella in amongst them."

"For their sake, I almost wish that was true. But I don't believe it, Mr. Felton." Billy shook his head sadly and stubbornly. "And even if that turns out to be the case, what difference does it make? This is still the work of Lobo's pack of curs and you all know it...Is everybody just going to accept it yet again? Or is there any among you who's man enough to ride in with me and confront them once and for all?"

"Now hold on," said his father sternly, gruffly. "I'm sorry if me and the other men here don't measure up to the fanciful idea of gun-blazing avengers you got out of some dime novel. But there's such a thing as reality. And the sorry fact we have to face, even if most of us don't like it any more than you do, is that the notion of us going against Lobo's Gun Wolves the way you're saying would be nothing short of suicide. The only thing it would accomplish would to be leave behind a bunch of widows and fatherless children. Is that what you want?"

"What I want is for those same children to see their fathers act like men!"

"That's enough! Your grief is making you talk crazy and you need to get hold of yourself," demanded the elder Doyle.

"Maybe I *am* crazy. But if I am," declared Billy, "I'd rather be that than just another mewling sheep waiting obediently for the next visit from the wolves. In the meantime...to hell with all of you!"

So saying, the lad spun on his heel and stomped away. In as much as he'd arrived with his parents in a buckboard and had just effectively eliminated leaving in the same manner, he continued stomping; departing in long, determined strides over the rolling hills without looking back.

"We should go after him, John," Mrs. Doyle said softly to her husband.

But Noah Felton, the white-whiskered old gent who

had spoken to Billy earlier, placed a work-gnarled hand on Doyle's arm and suggested instead, "Might be best to leave him be. He needs to be alone, wrestle with what he's feeling inside. The long, hard walk will help him do that, and I'm bettin' he'll be home for supper."

Gazing after his son with a forlorn look, Doyle said, "I hope so...But I ain't so sure."

CHAPTER SIXTEEN

IT WAS NEARLY DUSK WHEN THEY FINALLY ARRIVED IN Pickaxe, the Hightowers' rumbling, creaking wagon rolling between Lone and Velda plodding along on either side. With the pinkish gold glow of the setting sun starting to wrap soft, lengthening shadows around the buildings lining its main street, the place hardly looked like the menacing offshoot of Hell it was reported to be. In fact, the row of storefronts, both ones showing some age and others of more recent vintage, appeared universally well maintained, right down to freshly painted trim and swept boardwalks.

Activity on the street seemed to be waning with the close of the day, though most of the shops were still open. A ways up the street from the end where the new arrivals entered, two structures with more garishly painted fronts identifying them as saloons looked to be flourishing even as other trade was tapering off. The steady plinkety-plink of piano and banjo strains could be heard coming from within one or both.

Before going very far, though, Lone and the others came to a livery stable with some sprawl to it and a freshly whitewashed main barn that bespoke of a clean, well run operation.

Pulling back on the reins and bringing his rig to a halt in front of said barn, Reverend Hightower announced, "This appears a likely spot for us to bring our day to a close, friend McGantry and Miss Roxie. You two will probably want to go on and find yourselves hotel rooms but my daughter and I, as is our wont, will make arrangements to park our wagon and bed down here for the night. It's too late to try and work up a sermon any more this evening. In the morning, however, we will start posting notifications and hopefully have a gathering interested in hearing the word of the Lord by this time tomorrow afternoon."

"Sounds like you have it all planned out, Reverend," Lone replied. "Hope it goes well for you."

"As do I," Hightower said somewhat wistfully. Then he added, "Furthermore, if I recall correctly, by prior arrangement we should be able to count on seeing your faces in the crowd, should we not?"

"With the proviso," Velda reminded him, "we all last that long."

"Have faith, Miss Roxie. Have faith."

"The first thing I'm willin' to put some faith in," said Lone, "is that this looks like a decent place for us to put up our horses in addition to whatever arrangement you need to make for your wagon. So, let's go on in and do some business."

Together they climbed down from wagon and saddles and started for the barn. Emerging to meet them was a short, bow-legged, pot-bellied gent of more than a few years. He wore a welcoming smile under a mud-spattered derby hat with wisps of gray hair poking out from under its abbreviated brim. As he came forward, he kept the thumbs of each hand hooked behind the straps of bright red suspenders so that his bony elbows, poking out from the cut-off sleeves of his shirt, made Lone think of the wings on a plucked chicken.

"Evenin', folks," the sawed off suspenders-snapper greeted. "My name's Ebediah Wilkes and I run this establishment. If you're lookin' to board your horses and store your wagon, you came to the right place."

"That's close to what our needs are. Me and this young lady"—Lone tipped his head to indicate Velda—"are indeed lookin' to board our horses. The reverend and his daughter are seekin' something a bit different for them and their wagon, I'll let them explain."

Wilkes craned his neck and squinted to read the writing on the side of the wagon's canopy. "'Salvation. In ac–accor-dance to the word of the Lord'...Well, I'll be dogged. You *are* a preacher. Been a long time since we saw one of your kind in this town... er, Reverend."

"Then all the more reason for that to change, wouldn't you say?" responded Hightower.

"Makes no never mind to me," Wilkes allowed. "But I gotta tell you, there's some mighty rough hides hereabouts who might not be so willin' to be preached at about changin' their ways."

"Hardly the first time for that—going all the way back to the days of the Lord himself. But for the time being, let's just concern ourselves with the needs of my daughter and me regarding our wagon and animals ..." When the reverend went on to explain those needs—a place to park the wagon, with the understanding he and Hope would be staying in it, along with some graze and access to water for the horses—Wilkes proved very accommodating. He pointed out a grassy patch off one corner of a corral out behind the barn, and a nearby trough where the pulling team could be watered or from which buckets could be drawn. All at no charge. The businessman in him naturally tried to encourage the provision of some added grain or hay for the horses at a reasonable fee, but the frugality of the Hightowers negated that.

With that matter taken care of and the wagon on its way to the allotted grassy patch, Wilkes smilingly turned to the more profitable business represented by Lone and Velda. Once rates had been given and paid for the care of their animals, however, some questions were brought forth that the livery man didn't seem quite so eager to be involved with.

It started with Velda's inquiry of, "I came to Pickaxe seeking employment in one of Lobo Hines' establishments. Can you direct me to where I might find Mr. Hines?"

At first Wilkes looked somewhat startled. Then his expression turned into a scowl of uncertainty followed by disappointment and then a hint of disapproval. "Are you sure that's the name you're lookin' for, miss?"

"Quite. Is there a problem?" Velda asked coolly.

"No. No, I just wanted to make sure, that's all."

"Okay. Then here's something else you can be sure of—I'm well aware of Mr. Hines' reputation. The reputation of this whole town, for that matter. But I am an independent woman with every right to make my way as I see fit. And, not that it's any business of you or your dirty little mind, how I make my way is as an entertainer and hostess, nothing as tawdry as the gleam in your piggy little eyes suggests... Now I repeat: Do you or do you not know where I can find Lobo Hines?"

"The Gold Tip Hotel, down near the far end of the street," came the prompt answer. "Lobo owns it. Not that he don't own plenty more properties around town, but that's his prime one. He has both an apartment and a business office there...Though I don't know if the office is still open this late in the day. If Lobo ain't available, you maybe could ask for Miss Sarina."

"Sarina?"

"Sarina Lopez. She works with Lobo. Manages the Gold Tip and, from what I hear, she mostly handles the, uh, entertainment end of things. She stays at the Gold Tip, too."

Lone said, "This Gold Tip sounds like quite the joint. Me and Miss Drew will be looking for a place to stay while we're in town—Reckon we couldn't do much better than takin' rooms there, eh?"

Once again Wilkes' face went through some shifting expressions. "Well, uh, yeah...I mean, I guess. Sure ain't nobody I rub elbows with has ever stayed there. But it's no doubt the most high-toned place around...It's just that, er, the way I understand Lobo has mostly, uh, whatycall *exclusive* guests roomin' there."

"Exclusive?" Velda echoed.

"Look," Wilkes groaned in exasperation, "what goes on at the Gold Tip is way over my head and none of my business. I ought not be spoutin' off any more than I already have, okay? I don't want to say the wrong thing and make trouble for myself. You asked about findin' Lobo, best I know is to try at the Gold Tip."

"You risk makin' trouble for yourself just by answerin' some questions?" Lone prodded.

Wilkes fidgeted with his suspenders. "The lady said she knew about the reputation of Lobo and this town. Don't that hold true for you too? If so, you must have heard about his strict rules and the pack he calls the Gun Wolves who enforce 'em. You plan on stickin' around for very long, you better learn about 'em quick and then watch whatever you say and who you say it to."

Lone cocked an eyebrow. "Sounds an awful lot like what we call kowtowing' where I come from. Ain't something I ever been particularly good at."

"In that case, what you'd better be good at instead is usin' that iron strapped to your hip. Unless, since the lady's lookin' to work for Lobo, is that also your aim? To try and join the Wolves?"

"I already got a job. It's getting the lady safely this far. Beyond that," Lone grated, "I ain't made up my mind. But if and when I do, I don't see where it'll be any business of yours."

Wilkes finally took his thumbs out from behind his suspenders and held his hands up, palms facing out. "Take it easy, mister. Your business is yours, and none of mine."

"He's right, McGantry," said Velda. "We've badgered him plenty, I think that's enough."

"Okay," Lone allowed. "But just one more thing. This ain't badgerin', it's only a couple simple questions."

"Like what?" Wilkes wanted to know, looking suspicious.

"This black I'm turnin' in for you to board," Lone said with a jerk of his thumb. "I came by him in a roundabout way and ain't entirely happy with him. You have any stock on hand you're interested in sellin' or tradin'? I'd bargain mighty favorably for the right-lookin' animal."

Velda frowned. "You really have to go into that this minute?"

"Might as well take a look while we're right here," Lone told her. Then to the livery man: "How about it?"

Wilkes eyed the horse Lone had rode in on. "That ain't a bad lookin' animal you seem so anxious to get shed of. I'd trade for him if the deal was right and, yeah, I got stock for sale in the back corral. They're mixed in with some other horses I'm boardin', but I can point out which is which if you're interested in havin' a look. You can come along while I take your mounts back, have a gander to see if anything interests you."

Velda made little attempt to hide her lack of enthusiasm for the idea, but nevertheless gave an I-give-up shrug that signaled her acquiescence. With that, Wilkes turned and motioned for Lone and Velda to follow him into the barn. They did so, leading their horses until they got a quarter way down the building's wide center aisle where Wilkes called out to a young black man who was spreading fresh straw across the floor of an empty stall. "Take the horses from these fine folks, Hiram," he instructed. "Put up the saddles after they've taken their personal bags and such, then give the animals a good rubdown followed by a servin' of hay and grain. Once they've cleaned that up, we'll put 'em in the side corral for tonight. Make sure there's plenty of water in the tank out there."

"Will do, Mr. Wilkes," said Hiram.

He took the reins of the horses then waited for Lone and Velda to remove the personal gear they wanted to keep with them. While they were doing that, in as much as the light outside was fading and the inside of the barn was dimmer still, Wilkes lighted a lantern which he held high when they resumed walking the remaining length of the aisle. Reaching a set of sliding doors at the far end, the livery man pulled one of them back and revealed a gate that in turn opened to a broad rear corral where two dozen horses were milling about.

Though the light of dusk was still strong enough to give decent illumination, Wilkes propped his lantern up on a gate post and said, "There you are. Have yourself a look-see. A few of 'em belong to customers but about three quarters are mine to do with as I please. If you spot one that looks appealin', sing out and hopefully it's one we can talk a deal on."

But Lone didn't have to sing out.

That was taken care of by a sleek, deep-chested gray stallion from the middle of the pack who lifted his head, flared his nostrils, and did his own singing out with a sharp whinny. A moment later he was shouldering aside the other horses around him and breaking into an eager trot that brought him pounding over to the gate where Lone stood leaning with a wide grin on his face and a single word gushing out through it. "Ironsides!"

"Watch out for that one," Wilkes advised, taking a step back as he spoke. "He's been a might rank since the day he got here."

Ironsides pushed his nose through the gate rails and nuzzled its velvety softness against the side of Lone's face. Lone nuzzled back, still grinning. Then, turning to look at Wilkes, the grin faded and was replaced by a cold-eyed stare. Though clenched teeth, Lone grated, "Only time this big ol' gray acts rank is when he's been in company that deserves it—like the lowdown, not long for this world polecat who stole him from me!"

CHAPTER SEVENTEEN

Seated at his private table in an alcove of the Gold Tip Hotel dining room, Lobo Hines was preparing to cut into the succulent prime rib that had just been served to him when he glanced up and spotted the approach of a very anxious-looking Burt Kelson. As he drew nearer, Kelson's steps dragged with noticeable hesitancy.

Sharing Lobo's table was an elegantly beautiful woman with rich olive skin, glistening ebony hair piled intricately atop her head, and almond eyes the color of strong-brewed coffee with a touch of cream. Earrings like a cluster of icicles bracketed her chiseled face and her attire of a strapless ivory evening gown accentuated her long, graceful throat and displayed a tasteful hint of cleavage. Following the line of Lobo's gaze, her eyes touched briefly on Kelson, causing her to remark in a faint Spanish accent, "It appears your number one mongrel lacks the consideration to allow you even to eat in peace."

"He knows better than to bother me here unless it's something important," Lobo replied tersely. Then he raised a hand and motioned Kelson the rest of the way forward.

"Sorry to bust in on your supper, Boss," Kelson blurted as soon as he reached the edge of the table. "But I figured you wouldn't want to be kept waitin' to hear this."

"The wagon?" Lobo said, forging ahead to the obvious conclusion.

Kelson's head bobbed eagerly. "That's right. It rolled in not half an hour ago. Stopped down the street at Wilkes' livery."

"Still there now?"

"Far as I know. I sent Sam Long Eyes to keep watch on it."

"Does Dekker know it arrived?"

"Nope. I wanted to notify you first. I know where he's at though—playin' blackjack over a Red Lucy's. Want me to fetch him?"

"Yes. But watch what you say in front of anybody else. Tell him to come to my suite right away. Then round up a few other men—the ones you took with you out to the Milestone place this morning will do. Wait for Dekker and me out back."

"We goin' down to the livery?"

"That's the idea. Now get a move on."

Kelson spun on his heel and began weaving back out through the tables of the main dining room. Tuning to his lovely companion, Lobo said, "You, of course, know what this means, dear Sarina."

A ghost of a smile touched the woman's lush lips. "I should. I've been listening to you fret about it for weeks now."

"Well the fretting is over," Lobo assured her. "As you

heard, the wagon has at long last arrived so that puts us on the brink of achieving one mighty fine payday."

"Every day is payday for you," Sarina pointed out. "You have dozens of different revenue streams all through town, and even sometimes beyond."

"Yeah, but they're all fluctuating dribs and drabs compared to this single punch. Plus," Lobo added with a scheming gleam in his eyes, "if I play my cards right, I figure I have a better than fifty-fifty chance of getting that greedy red fool Toneka to reveal the source of the gold he'll be paying me with. Then, after him and his wild-eyed followers have gone on their rampage and ultimately been once again ground under the hooves and bootheels of the army troops that will be called in, I may still know where to get my hands on more of that lovely yellow stuff dreams are made of."

Sarina arched a brow and said dryly, "Oh, yes. Because hauling gold out of territory claimed by the Indians has worked out so well for so many others who've tried it. A few years back, I believe a gentleman named Custer served as a good example by paying a rather heavy price for representing interests from back east who thought along similar lines."

"Custer was a fool and those who set him up were too greedy and heavy-handed," Lobo chuffed. "Trust me, I'm a lot smarter than that."

"I do trust you, darling," Sarina said, reaching over to place her palm lightly on the back of his hand.

Lobo, in turn, brought the palm of his other hand across to cup over the back of hers. "Good. Then you'll trust and understand when I say this matter is important enough to require me leaving your company and going to tend to it right away."

"Certainly. I will have Paul make some sandwiches out of your prime rib and leave them wrapped and waiting in your suite for when you return. I likely will be in my quarters by then. Let me know when you get back."

Lobo stood to leave. "What about the girl, the preacher's daughter. How's she doing?"

Sarina shrugged. "Physically, she's fine. She eats and cleanses herself when no one is around. At every little sound and the mere sight of anyone, however, she shrinks back and cowers like a beaten puppy even though no one has ever laid a hand on her. If she didn't have that Bible she constantly clutches to herself, I fear she could actually go a little mad just from the fright of whatever she imagines might happen to her."

"Well, keep her as presentable as you can. I might need her before this is over. It won't be much longer now."

"I put the two new girls, the Milestone sisters, in with her for now. My thought was that it might help put all of them a little more at ease for the time being." Sarina paused, frowning. "But the minister's daughter, Hope—you don't intend to truly return her to the father, do you? And I'm convinced she could never endure the strain of, well, being put to another use."

"I might have to use her to complete the deal with her old man, that's what I meant about maybe needing her and why I want her presentable for the short term. After that ..." Lobo made a blunt throwaway gesture. "And if she can't measure up for anything else, that'll be her tough luck. As for the other two, though—the Milestone sisters—I expect to see them conditioned and made ready as usual."

"I will see to it. As usual."

"WELL YOU'VE REALLY GONE and done it, McGantry!" Velda fumed. "This stunt with that blasted horse of yours is about to blow the lid off all the plans we made. Like throwing a hot coal in a powder keg! Didn't you for one second stop to think about that?"

"Maybe not. Maybe the sight of Ironsides caused me to lose my cool," Lone conceded with a sour expression. "On the other hand, maybe what I did was just hurry us along toward what our goal was anyway. What was the point of all that finaglin' we had mapped out—you playin' a saloon floozy, me worryin' about passin' Lobo's smell test? It was for you to flush out Mitchum and for me to find my stolen horse, right? So this way is goin' at the same things, only in reverse. I got my horse and now we can use me re-claimin' him as the way to flush out Mitchum."

"That might be all fine and dandy except for what you call *re-claiming* is almost certainly going to be seen as plain old horse stealing by everybody else," Velda argued. "When that livery man goes running to report what you did, which he's bound to do, it's the town's Gun Wolf enforcers, not Mitchum, who'll be coming to look for you. Wilkes never heard Mitchum's name, not even an alias. All he knew was that a Gold Tip servant brought in Ironsides for boarding and said he belonged to one of the hotel's 'exclusive' guests. Could be this little escapade of yours won't stand a chance of drawing Mitchum out at all—not if the Gun Wolves come swarming first to take care of us. Mitchum might not hear anything until it's all over."

"That's why we ain't wastin' no time headin' for the Gold Tip," Lone explained. "We're gonna find the servant who took Ironsides to the livery and make him identify the exclusive guest the horse supposedly belonged to. Then we'll pay a visit to Mr. Exclusive—who we figure has to be Mitchum, tucked away in one of Lobo's high rent hideout rooms—and make sure he knows we're in town and what our intentions are."

Velda arched a brow skeptically. "You make paying that visit sound mighty easy. From my saddle, just making it as far as that fancy hotel way up the street looks like enough room to give us trouble before we even get there."

Said street, Pickaxe's main drag called Center Street, was what they were riding right down the middle of. Velda on her same mount as always; Lone now once again on his beloved Ironsides. Having spotted the big gray in Wilkes' corral, there'd been no holding back for Lone. He damn sure wasn't going to leave his old friend behind and risk losing track of him again while continuing the pursuit of Mitchum. So, standing firm on that decision and impulsively re-taking possession of Ironsides by force from Wilkes was what propelled things to the point they'd now reached—him and Velda headed for the Gold Point, hell bent on cornering Mitchum there and then facing whatever consequences came as a result.

As they continued up the street, their eyes swept alertly from side to side, noting the diminishing activity in the deepening shadows as more and more shops closed for the evening yet only a few outside lamps were so far lighted. Velda, who even though she had ditched her saloon floozy persona and resignedly changed back to her trail attire complete with gunbelt openly strapped on, wasn't done expressing concerns about some specifics of what they were embarked upon. "In the first place, if we do make it that far, we're going to have to deal with whatever security Lobo has set up at the hotel. His whole reputation, remember, is based on providing a safe haven for fugitives on the run. And the Gold Tip obviously represents the top of the line, the safest haven of all for those wanted the most and willing to pay the most...In other words, getting at Mitchum there, even with a crazy bold play like the one we're making, isn't going to be easy."

"Don't recall 'easy' ever figurin' in on any of the plans we had for pullin' this off," Lone countered.

"No. But suicide was never figured in either."

Ignoring that, Lone said, "Okay, that was your 'in the first place'—you got any more?"

"Oh, I've got plenty more. But let's cut to the big finish. Say we succeed in getting our hands on Mitchum. By that point, every Gun Wolf in town is certain to be on alert to stop us. You happen to have a plan for how we're going to blast our way clear of them?"

"There it is. You just named the plan," Lone declared. "Comes time, we'll blast our way straight through that pack of vermin-ridden mongrels!"

CHAPTER EIGHTEEN

Ebediah Wilkes was in a highly agitated state. He knew he'd done nothing wrong, done all he reasonably could to prevent any wrong from taking place—yet at the same time he feared he would share in the blame for what had occurred. Having any horse stolen from his livery was bad enough; but having it belong to one of the *exclusive* guests from Lobo Hines' Gold Tip Hotel was bad to an extreme degree.

Wilkes had known immediately, of course, that he would have to report the theft—either directly to someone at the hotel or preferably to Burt Kelson if he could find him relatively quick. It had only been a matter of needing to take some time to carefully formulate the best way to present the sequence of events that ended with the unidentified stranger claiming the big gray stallion was his stolen property and riding off on him. Wilkes had naturally tried to argue the point but the steel in the stranger's eyes and the .44 riding on his hip in a manner that suggested he knew how to use it, kept the livery man's protests from being very forceful.

That left the troublesome question, the thing that slowed Wilkes in charging out to make his report, of whether or not Lobo or whoever the guest was who'd first rode in on the gray would believe he'd put up sufficient resistance.

And now, startlingly, the whole thing came racing to a point of immediacy when Wilkes looked around and saw, entering through the side door of his barn, none other than Lobo Hines himself, followed by Burt Kelson and four other men. It seemed impossible they could somehow already know what happened and arrive so fast in response, but Wilkes could think of no other reason for them showing up here.

Before the livery man could stammer any kind of greeting, Lobo barked gruffly, "Where is it?"

Somewhat baffled, Wilkes said, "The horse? I – I don't know. The stranger rode out of here on him a few minutes ago. Him and the woman turned up the street toward—"

"What the hell are you talking about a horse and some stranger and a woman?" Lobo cut him off. "I want to know about the wagon—the goddamned preacher's wagon you got parked somewhere around here!"

After leaving the hotel dining room, Lobo had gone to his suite and changed from dinner jacket and dress shoes to the whipcord jacket and boots he now had on. When Dekker joined him, as summoned, he'd been quickly updated on the long-awaited arrival of the wagon and then the two of them had gone down the back stairs to join with Kelson and the other three Gun Wolves he'd rounded up—Lasko, Jess Philbin, and Evan "Even Dozen" Dozier (so named because of the twin pistols he carried, each with a fully loaded wheel providing an even dozen rounds always at his disposal).

In as much as Lobo wanted to maintain a measure of discretion regarding his interest in the wagon (and especially its cargo), he'd led his contingent down the back sides of the various businesses lining Pickaxe's main street until they reached Wilkes' livery and entered through the side door of the barn. Standing there now, he repeated, "The goddamned wagon, Wilkes— where is it?"

Still clearly bewildered, Wilkes said, "The wagon? It's, uh, it's over on the other side of the barn. In a lot off the corner of the corral. The minister and his daughter are still with it...But the other two who came with them, the woman and the fella who took off with the gray horse—"

"There you go with the stupid horse again!" This time it was Kelson who cut him off. "Didn't you hear Mr. Hines tell you it's the wagon he's interested in?"

"Okay, I got that," Wilkes responded, a bit more sharply now since he was addressing Kelson and not Lobo directly. "I answered where to find it. But, if you'll listen a minute, I think it's also important you let me tell you about those other two and the horse the man stole —since it belongs to one of Mr. Hines' guests at the Gold Tip."

Lobo, having started for where they'd been told they would find the wagon, stopped short and turned back. "What did you just say? What horse—belonging to which one of my hotel guests?"

"I–I don't know exactly." Wilkes withered once more under Lobo's fierce glare. "All I know is one of the hotel servants brought him in a couple of days ago, a handsome gray stallion this stranger shows up and all of a sudden starts clamorin' actually belongs to him. Next thing I know..." From there, Wilkes quickly related the whole incident, trying not to stammer too much in the telling, just wanting to get it out and get it over with. All the while, in the back of his mind, he was hoping that whatever had Lobo so anxious about the wagon might work to divert some of the anger he might otherwise focus wholly on the horse theft.

As soon as Wilkes was done, it appeared his wish was at least partially granted. The first reaction out of Lobo was a stern look directed at Kelson rather than the livery man. "These two—the man and woman this babbling fool is describing—do they sound like the same strangers you saw at the Milestone place earlier today? The ones you judged as not being particularly worrisome?"

Kelson grimaced. "Yeah...I reckon it must be," he allowed.

"It appears your judgment was damn well off the mark." Lobo smacked a balled fist against the side of his leg. Spinning on Wilkes, he snarled, "None of this leaves you off the hook, you worthless sniveler! You're supposed to protect the property put in your care—especially property directly or indirectly connected to me."

"I did everything I could, Mr. Hines. Honest," Wilkes insisted. "But the man and the woman both were heeled by the time they rode out of here. And me without no kind of gun anywhere in reach, there just wasn't—"

"Shut up! You were no good then, you're even more useless to be of any help now. Did you at least see which way they went?" Lobo asked.

"They turned up the street...T-toward the Gold Point, it looked like."

Lobo cut another hard look back to Kelson. "I'll give you a chance to square things for that lousy judgment you made. I've got more important business to tend to with the wagon. You take Even Dozen and Long Eyes... Where the hell is that 'breed, anyway? I thought you said you left him watching things?"

"Watchin' the wagon, not things here in the barn," Kelson replied. "He's out there, you can count on it."

"He'd better be. Take him and Even Dozen, like I said. That should be enough. Go run down that horse thieving bastard. Shoot him if he don't give you any choice, but take him alive if you can. Been a while since we've treated the town to a good hanging, he'll help quench everybody's thirst."

"What about the woman?" Kelson wanted to know.

"You said she was pretty, right?"

"Real pretty."

Lobo sneered. "Then do you really need to ask?"

OUT FRONT of the livery barn, as Lobo and the others turned toward where the wagon was parked, Kelson stepped to the edge of the street with Even Dozen at his side and called out, "Strong Eyes! Where you at?"

In response, silently reverse melting out of the shadows on the opposite side of the street, a man appeared. He held a Henry repeating rifle diagonally across his chest, fore stock resting lightly in the crook of his left am. He was hatless, the crown of his head shaved bare, and was clad in a loose-fitting buckskin shirt and baggy trousers. The high cheekbones and sharp nose of his facial features clearly identified the fact he had some Indian blood in him.

As he came nearer, Kelson said, "You didn't make nothing of the ruckus that went on here a little bit ago?"

Strong Eyes shrugged and then answered in much the same way Kelson had responded to Lobo. "Some men were arguing in the barn. White men are always arguing about something, so I paid no attention. You told me to watch the wagon and the people with it—where they were, everything was quiet."

"Yeah, well, I guess that much is okay," Kelson had to admit grudgingly. "But the argument in the barn, as I reckon you saw, ended up with a man riding off on a big gray stud."

Strong Eyes nodded. "Yes, a man and woman rode off. The gray horse was not the one the man came in on."

"Uh-huh. And that's the problem. The troublemaker *claims* the horse is his, see," Kelson explained, "but it's not. So he stole it. And the person the nag truly belongs to is a guest at Lobo's hotel."

"Meanin' Mr. Lobo wants the horse back pronto and wants the snake who took it run down and stomped—by us," added Even Dozen with an eager gleam in his eyes.

"So did you pay attention where he went?" Kelson asked Strong Eyes.

"Easy," the 'breed grunted. He stretched out an arm and pointed. "Him and the woman went straight up the street. See them? They've almost reached the Gold Tip."

CHAPTER NINETEEN

HARLAN HIGHTOWER ROSE FROM BESIDE THE CAMPFIRE over which he had a pot of coffee just beginning to boil and watched impassively as the girl who'd been pretending to be his daughter for the past three weeks —Hilary Banks, she'd told him, was her real name—ran forward and threw herself wantonly into the arms of one of the four men who came striding boldly into their camp. Hightower recognized the man as Mel Dekker, the ruthless scoundrel who'd taken Hope, his true daughter, from him and used her to force his participation in the scheme about to be finally concluded.

The reverend had never laid eyes on any of the other men before yet he had no trouble marking one of them, by how he carried himself and the way he'd marched in a couple steps ahead of the rest, as the notorious Lobo Hines. Helping to confirm this, the man proceeded straight to Hightower, ignoring the prolonged embrace of Hilary and Dekker, and said, "I see you finally made it with my delivery, preacher man."

"The only delivery I make willingly is the word of

the Lord," Hightower replied, meeting Lobo's flat gaze. "But if you're referring to the other cargo forced on me by your man Dekker and the girl Hilary, then yes that is also in the wagon."

Half of Lobo's mouth lifted in a humorless smile. "That's just swell, Preach. You hang on to the word of the Lord, I'll take the other off your hands."

Hilary untangled herself from Dekker's arms and turned to say, "You'll find what you want under the boxes of Bibles—six flat crates of Winchester 78s, a dozen rifles and five hundred cartridges to a crate."

"Music to my ears," Lobo declared, his smile widening for real.

"There are some lanterns hanging on the rear of the wagon you can light in order to see better," Hilary added.

Lobo motioned to Lesko and Philbin. "You heard the lady. Snap to it. Get those lanterns lit and the crates dug out and pried opened so I can see what I've been waiting too damn long for."

As the two Wolves moved to the rear of the wagon, Hightower kept his gaze fixed on Lobo and said in a tightly controlled tone, "What about my daughter?"

"What do you mean?" Lobo responded mockingly.

"I mean where is she? Is she okay? The deal was that she'd be returned to me if I got your wretched guns through!"

Lobo heaved a sigh. "Relax, Preach. Your daughter is fine. As soon as the guns are uncrated and I see that everything is okay, I'll have her trotted out."

"You got no worry about the guns, Lobo," said Hilary, stepping away from Dekker and moving closer. "They're just fine. Mel and me saw them go into the crates and I haven't been more than a few yards away from them or that lousy wagon since the lids got tacked on."

"Truthfully spoken," Hightower proclaimed in a somewhat surprising show of support. "You fellows" —a tip of his head to Lobo and then Dekker— "should be very proud of Hilary's devotion to duty. There's obviously not much I can approve of about this whole operation, but there's no denying how hard she worked to hold up her end."

Hilary lifted her brows and smiled uncertainly. "That's decent of you to say, Fa—oops, I guess I can quit calling you my father now. Still, it was nice of you to—"

"Knock it off, for crying out loud," Dekker objected. "Who cares what this sky pilot thinks? Whatya gonna do next, toss some money in his collection plate?"

"The thing about it," Hightower continued calmly, ignoring Dekker's lament, "was that Hilary's dedication all through those long, hard days on the trail—something she wasn't used to—left her very exhausted come nightfall."

"So what are you getting at?" Hilary wanted to know, scowling suspiciously.

"What I'm getting at," the reverend told her, "is that exhausted people tend to sleep very deeply. Deeply enough so that even though they may be only a few yards away from certain activity, their slumber can still go quite undisturbed by it."

By now Hilary and Dekker and Lobo, all three, were scowling suspiciously. "If you got some kind of point to make, Preach," growled Lobo, "get to it and be quick about it."

"Okay. My point is this: If you thought for one

second I was naive enough to trust that you would honor the deal to release my daughter to me and then let the two of us safely go after I brought in these guns, then you are by far a bigger bunch of fools than you took me for." Hightower's voice rose to a low boom and his eyes were blazing. "Those rifles your men are unpacking will look to be in fine shape at first appearance. But a slightly closer examination will reveal they are in fact useless—because I removed the firing pin from each and every one!"

"That's a lie!" Hilary exclaimed. "There's no way you could have accomplished that without me knowing. And how could a preacher even know enough about guns to pull a trick like that?"

Hightower smiled slyly. "I wasn't born a preacher, gal. I grew up around guns on a hardscrabble Indiana farm, learned to shoot and hunt in order to help put food on our family's table from the time I was eight. In the late war, I learned how to dismantle and un-jam a rifle in the dark, the rain, and the hell of battle—conditions that ended up turning me to the ministry. But that didn't make me forget what I knew about firearms."

"I still say you're lying!"

"Keep believing that if you want." Hightower shrugged. "But you've only got a couple minutes before the first crate is open and then you won't be able to deny it anymore."

Hilary and Dekker broke away and rushed toward where the first crate was being dragged down from the wagon bed.

Lobo remained standing in front of Hightower. Slowly, he slipped his hand inside the vest under his whipcord jacket and drew the short-barreled Colt Lightning from it. He aimed this at the reverend from near point-blank range, saying, "If that was some lame attempt at creating a diversion so you could make a break for it, I guess you can see it failed miserably."

"Attempting an escape—at least at this juncture—is the farthest thing from my mind," the reverend assured him. "I don't plan on going anywhere until I have my daughter safely beside me."

"And you think a double-crossing trick like this is the best way to get what you want?"

The muscles at the hinges of Hightower's jaw bulged. "I think it's the only way. You see, those firing pins are hidden, buried, at a spot back on the trail where you'll never find them without me. It's a spot with good visibility for miles in every direction so I can be sure we aren't followed. By 'we' I mean you, me, and my daughter. When I'm satisfied we are in the clear, I'll reveal where your precious pins are and we can then go our separate ways."

"You'll never get away with it!" Lobo hissed.

"Maybe not. But if I don't, neither will you ever get those rifles in a usable condition."

Over behind the wagon, sudden furor was breaking out. Coming from the knot of shifting, shadowy shapes on the fringe of lantern glow could be heard the sound of ripping wood and the thump and clatter of rifles being pulled free from one of the crates. Then came more clattering followed quickly by a growing chorus of curses. Everything but the report of a rifle discharging.

"Damn it all!" bellowed Dekker, flinging down a Winchester in frustration and reaching to seize another. "I think the sneaky bastard actually did it. Even with fresh loads, none of these are firing!"

"Open more crates! Make sure!" Lobo ordered.

Lesko and Philbin promptly pulled another crate down from the wagon and began tearing away the lid. While they were doing that, Dekker failed once again to get a discharge from the latest rifle he'd grabbed. Emitting a half-strangled curse, he spun around and came rushing toward where Lobo and Hightower stood.

"Damn you to hell!" he seethed as he raised the Winchester he still gripped and thrust forward with its butt, slamming it hard against the reverend's forehead. Hightower staggered back, issuing a loud grunt of surprise and pain and then collapsed to the ground. Dekker followed, taking a stance over him, once more raising the rifle, ready to strike again. "I put too much into this to let you and your slippery tricks foul it up at the last minute!"

But before Dekker could bring the rifle down, Lobo stepped into him with a sudden backhand sweep of one arm and sent him stumbling aside. "Hold on, you damn fool," he snarled. "We need to keep him alive in order to find out where he hid those firing pins!"

"Okay, okay. I wasn't gonna kill him," Dekker said sullenly. "And if you want to find out about the pins, let me at him. I got plenty of ways to make a man talk."

Lobo frowned. "Maybe you do, maybe you don't. But these sky pilot types get some awful strong will power from their faith. Remember all those ancient Christians who marched unfaltering right into the jaws of lions."

"Yeah, I read those storybooks when I was a kid too. But—"

Dekker stopped short at the sudden sound of gunfire. Not from any of the recently delivered rifles, unfortunately, but from a distance; somewhere up the main street of town.

"That better be the sound of Kelson and the others catching up with that lowdown, stinkin' horse thief," Lobo said through clenched teeth. "At least it would mean one of this evening's problems is getting settled..."

CHAPTER TWENTY

Lone and Velda reined up in front of the Gold Tip Hotel. It was an impressive structure, the largest and newest of any they'd passed anywhere along the street. Three stories tall, every inch of it whitewashed to the point it almost gleamed even in the waning light. Pillars bracketed the thick, polished oak door of the front entrance. High glass windows stretched to either side. Through those on the right could be seen an elegant, brightly illuminated dining room; to the left was revealed a smoky, more dimly lighted barroom.

"Pretty high-toned shack for housing some of the scurviest human dregs in the West," remarked Velda as she gave it a good looking over.

"Uh-huh," Lone allowed. "And, by the way, did you happen to notice we made it this far without any trouble?"

"I'll give you that much," said Velda. "But there's still room for the old saying about the calm before the storm."

Barely more than a second later, as if to prove her

words prophetic, the front door burst open and four men emerged in a rough entanglement. Two of the men were tall, massive-shouldered bruisers in matching swallow-tailed jackets, gray in color with black piping, and wine red ties cinched incongruously around their tree stump necks. Flailing and struggling in their grasp were two average-sized hombres clad in the well-worn attire of working wranglers.

"You dirty, dusty damn cowboys have been told time and again," growled one of the bruisers, roughly shaking the individual he had hold of and doing so with apparent ease. "The Gold Tip bar is for men of prominence and their lady companions—not for rannies like you who don't even bother to scrape the horseshit off your boots before you try coming in!"

The speaker, his face purpled by anger, was a bullet-headed specimen, clean shaven and with a cap of reddish hair clipped so close it looked like brush bristles no more than a quarter-inch in length. The unfortunate gent on the receiving end of both the tirade and the rough handling looked to be a fairly young man in his middle twenties, in need of a shave and with an untrimmed shock of sun-bleached hair that was flopping around like the strings of a mop.

The other bouncer—for that's what the two monkey-suited fellows clearly were—had a neatly trimmed beard and slicked back brown hair. Without words, he was man-handling the second cowboy just as roughly and with equal ease. This victim appeared to have some years on his partner, was a bit leaner in build, with a few flecks of gray in his beard stubble and a thinning head of hair, though what there was still being shaken into disarray.

As if on cue, the bouncers suddenly released their grips on the cowboys, leaving them to lurch and stagger before grabbing hold of one another in order to regain their balance and keep from falling down.

The bullet-headed bouncer thrust out an arm and pointed to the pair, saying, "Alright, you've been warned and you got off lucky by only being slapped around a little bit. You come back again, you ain't gonna be so lucky and I guarantee you won't walk away on your own power."

That should have been the end of it. But when the two bouncers turned to go back inside, the younger cowboy showed himself to be too foolhardy (likely due to having had too much to drink somewhere earlier) to let it go.

"Too hell with that!" he shouted at the retreating broad backs. "This is a free country and a body has a right to drink wherever he pleases, as long as he can pay the freight. My money is honest-earned by hard work and sweat, makin' it just as good to spend in your fancy-assed joint as that of any oily-palmed businessman!"

The bearded bouncer glanced over his shoulder and said, "The problem ain't with your money—it's with you, you hay-brained piece of ranch trash."

Responding with a howl of rage, the young cowboy shoved away from his partner and lunged after the bouncers. In practiced unison, the two big men spun back around to face him. They met his charge first with a meaty fist pounded hard into his stomach by the bearded one and then, when the cowboy doubled over, a knee from Bullet Head jerked up savagely to slam into his face as it dropped downward. From where they sat their horses, Lone and Velda could hear the crunch of nose cartilage mixed with the sound of the blow impacting.

Even as the driving knee snapped his head up and back, the cowboy's own knees buckled and he began to tip to one side. But the bearded bouncer grabbed him by the shoulders and wouldn't let him drop. He jerked the young man upright, but only long enough to drill home another gut punch. Bullet Head was waiting to once more deliver a follow-up, but this time a slashing elbow uppercut that sent blood flying from the smashed nose and turned the cowboy's whole body as limp as a piece of rope.

"That's enough, you bastards!" wailed the older cowboy.

The bearded bouncer swiveled his head and said with a taunting smile, "You want some, too, old man? Come right on ahead."

All of a sudden Lone had skinned off Ironsides' back and was moving forward in long strides. "No, the old fella don't want none," he said in answer to the taunt. "And I think the young one's had enough."

He kept moving forward even as two fierce glares bored into him.

"*You* think?" echoed Bullet Head. "What makes you think anybody should give a damn what—"

He stopped short at the sight of Lone's .44 suddenly appearing in his fist, its muzzle moving in a slow, steady arc back and forth between the pair of punishers. "If there's any brains between those ears of yours," grated the former scout, "you should be smart enough to see I got six pretty good reasons right here for you to give a damn what I think."

"And if that's not enough, I got six more," said Velda,

leaning forward in the saddle and reaching casually across its horn to aim her own Colt.

The bearded bouncer's mouth dropped open in disbelief. "You two gotta be loco, drawin' on us. You know who we are—who we work for?"

Lone answered, "All I know is what you're gonna be if you don't let go of that boy, easy-like, and allow his pard to help him."

"Sure. Go ahead and take him. What's left," sneered Bullet Head. "And while you're at it, take a real good look...Because that's just a taste of what you're gonna look like after Lobo Hines gets wind of you interfering with us doing our job."

"Go on and do it then. Why not be the one to make sure Lobo finds out?" Lone challenged as the older cowboy got his sagging pal's arm over his shoulders and helped him stay on his feet long enough to pull back from the duo who had done the damage to him. "I been hearing about the big bad wolf ever since I hit town—trot him out, I'm anxious to meet him."

"Talk like that is gonna introduce you to a pine box and a six-foot hole in the ground," warned Bullet Head.

Before Lone could respond, a new voice suddenly entered the fray. It came in the form of a shout ringing out from back down the street, behind Lone.

"Hey! Everybody up there hold it! What the hell's goin' on? You with the guns—drop 'em and be quick about it!"

The voice sounded both threatening and vaguely familiar but Lone was reluctant to divert his attention from the already present threat of the two bouncers right in front of him.

Velda solved this dilemma by telling him to "Keep

'em covered" while she twisted around in her saddle for a look behind. Her report of what she saw was far from good news. "Damn! It looks like the storm I said might be due after the calm is about to arrive, McGantry. That oaf Kelson we saw out at the Milestone farm this morning is coming up the street. He's got two others with him, and they're all waving guns."

"Means we damn sure ain't droppin' ours!" declared Lone. Then: "Let's switch—you keep your hogleg trained on these two muscleheads while I have another chat with Kelson."

"Don't worry about us, we ain't going nowhere," crowed Bullet Head. "I wouldn't miss this show for anything."

Velda nevertheless twisted back around in the saddle and leveled her sights on the two bouncers once again while Lone turned his attention to the men coming up the street. Dusk was thickening fast and there was still only a smattering of lanterns glowing on either side to offset it. But it was enough for Lone to plainly make out Kelson. One of the men with him—lean and lanky, packing twin holsters with the shooting iron from one of them already drawn—Lone also recognized from this morning. The third hardcase he'd never seen before, but his facial features indicated a dose of Indian blood and the way he was holding a Henry rifle at the ready indicated he wouldn't hesitate to put the weapon to use.

"That's about close enough, Kelson," Lone called with the trio at half a block's distance. He took a step forward, the .44 held at his waist and centered on the Wolf lieutenant.

"I ain't in the habit of takin' orders from no snake

low horse thief. 'Specially when I got a three-to-one bulge on him," snorted Kelson. Yet, even as he said it, he and the other two came to a shuffling halt.

"I wouldn't be so quick to dismiss my partner," Lone advised. "But even if we leave it three-to-one like you said, you can see where this shooter of mine is already aimed. Lead starts flyin', it won't miss you no matter what else happens."

A corner of Kelson's left eye ticked ever so slightly before he sneered, "So you figure we got us a Mexican stand-off, eh? Only trouble with that is, we're a long way from Mexico and there ain't a damn greaser in sight."

"Shakes out the same, no matter what you call it," Lone countered.

"I say it shakes out he's bluffin' his ass off," said the punk with two guns. "Let's just go ahead and cut him in two, Kelse. Lobo will have to find somebody else to hang."

Lone smiled coldly. "You got a real brave soldier there, Lieutenant... Willin' to let you take my first bullet while bankin' him or the 'breed can put me down before I get to them."

"The point is, you *are* goin' down," Kelson insisted. "You ain't got a chance."

"In that case, I guess the kid's right. We might as well cut to it," said Lone. "But savor the thought now, because no matter if I bite the dust you ain't gonna be around to enjoy it afterward."

Everything seemed to go silent and still all up and down the street and there was nothing but the flinty stares passing between Lone and Kelson ...

Until, suddenly, bursting out from a side street at the end of the block behind Kelson and his men, came a figure on horseback spurring his mount furiously and shouting into the tense silence. “No! You’re mine, Kelson! Mine, you murderous, girl-stealing scum! First you and then Lobo—tonight’s the night all of you are gonna pay!”

CHAPTER TWENTY-ONE

THE APPEARANCE OF THE MYSTERIOUS RIDER BROKE THE tension-locked scene wide open. Around the corner he came tearing, a long object thrusting out from one hand, his horses' hooves throwing dust and clods of dirt as they dug to make the turn and then go charging straight for the men in the middle of the street.

After a moment's hesitation, the rataplan rushing up from behind forced Kelson to turn away from Lone and spin to see who was attacking and cursing him. Even quicker to turn, however, was Sam Strong Eyes, swinging his Henry rifle around as he did. Seeing this, the approaching horseman used the long object he was holding to make a stabbing motion in the half breed's direction that resulted in the fiery flash and roar of a shotgun's discharge. The impact of the twelve gauge load lifted Strong Eyes off the ground, hurtled him four feet through the air, and then slammed him down again in a limp, dead sprawl, the Henry clattering away out of his grasp.

Still charging forward, the horseman swung his

shotgun in a flat arc and brought it to bear on Kelson as the Wolf lieutenant was completing his own turn and raising a pistol to aim in defense. But before either man could shoot, "Even Dozen" Dozier triggered a round that tore upward through the shoulder of the mounted shotgunner. The latter's second barrel discharged an instant later, simultaneous with Kelson snapping off a shot. But the rider's body jerk caused by taking the bullet from Dozier resulted in two misses—the shotgun blast gouging the street half a foot off target, Kelson's slug ripping nothing but air an equal distance errant.

From where he stood, Lone didn't wait for any of the three involved in that exchange to make another try. He got off the next shot, choosing two-gun Dozier for his target. He scored a hit, though lower than intended. His bullet punched into the lanky gunman's right thigh, spinning him half around and dropping him to one knee with a yelp of pain.

Satisfied that he'd at least preoccupied the gunman for a time, Lone shifted his attention to Kelson. Or he tried. What he found was that he was unable to get a clear shot at the man because the horseman had ridden up too close. Apparently having no back-up weapon and electing not to take time to try and reload his shotgun, the rider was trying to run down the Wolf lieutenant with his horse while at the same time slashing viciously at him with the barrels of the emptied blaster. For his part, Kelson was darting and dodging to avoid the horse and flailing his arms above his head to block being struck by the heavy gun.

In frustration, Lone broke into a run toward the embroiled pair, firing a shot skyward in hopes of disrupting things before Kelson found an opening of his own to use the pistol still in his hand and plant a near point-blank round into his attacker.

As Lone surged to try and handle that, Velda suddenly found herself with more to deal with than holding at bay the two bouncers under her gun. Directly behind the pair, the Gold Point's front door popped open and a blur of faces and bodies from inside—drawn by the sound of gunfire out in the street—tried to swarm out with shouts of: "What's going on?" "What's happening?"

"Kelson's in trouble out in the street," Bullet Head blurted in response.

That's all Velda allowed time for. "Stay inside—mind your own business!" she hollered as she triggered a round from her Colt that drilled a walnut-sized hole in the partially open door. Those on the other side fell back with startled yelps.

In front, the two bruisers held out their meaty palms and wailed as one voice, "Not us, not us! We don't go heeled!"

"Then maybe it's time you start!" Velda suggested. For emphasis, she fired twice more in quick succession, blowing apart the brightly burning lanterns placed high above each corner of the hotel's front door. Glass shards and flaming coal oil exploded outward and then splattered even wider upon hitting the ground. The tall, gleaming white pillars almost immediately had flames licking up around their bases. In the midst of this, the two bouncers wheeled about and bulled their way back inside as frantically as if they feared the swallowtails of their fancy jackets would be the next to catch.

This fiery tableau was enough to create the momentary disruption Lone had been trying for in the struggle between Kelson and his attacker. Trouble was, it also made a brief opening for Kelson to finally get off a shot. Lone heard the muffled report and saw the rider slump in his saddle. A second later Lone reached them and slammed a shoulder into Kelson, sending him staggering. But before he could attempt any kind of follow-up, Dozier got back in on the action and sent a slug sizzling through the air mere inches in front of Lone's nose.

The former scout dropped low and reached across his body to blindly trigger return fire. He came close enough to make Dozier crab away on his wounded leg, seeking a pool of deep shadows at the edge of the street. While Lone wasted another shot, chasing him into the blackness, Kelson darted the other way and ran for shadows on the opposite side of the street.

Up in front of the hotel, Velda had holstered her nearly spent Colt and drawn her Winchester from its saddle scabbard. Levering a round into the chamber, she turned in her saddle with a look of concern on her pretty face and shouted, "You'd better do something quick, McGantry! I think the hornets are about to swarm a lot thicker!"

Right on cue, the windows of the Gold Tip barroom began bursting outward and the snouts of rifles and pistols could be seen poking through.

Lone reached up to steady the rider now sagging in his saddle, saying, "Whoever you are, you crazy fool, you got any strength left to ride?"

The pain-etched face of the rider looked down at him and Lone was startled to see it belonged to young Billy Doyle, the tormented youth who'd stomped away from the Milestone funeral earlier that day. "I can ride for as long as it takes to finish the job of killing Kelson and Lobo!" he declared.

"First things first," Lone told him. "And right now that means stayin' alive long enough to get away from here. So hang on!" Grabbing the reins of Billy's horse and dragging him along, Lone began running back to the hotel.

By this time, Velda—joined somewhat surprisingly by the two cowboys who'd been roughed up by the bouncers—was trading shots with men firing from the barroom window. Lone burned some powder in the same cause, emptying the rounds left in his .44 as he ran. Reaching Ironsides, he sprang into the saddle, still gripping Billy's reins. "One of you men take over here," he called to the cowboys. "Climb up behind this kid and hang on to him, he's hurt. The other one of you swing up behind me."

"Where we goin'?" asked the older of the pair even as he and his battered partner were moving forward as bid.

"The hell away from here!" came Lone's answer.

"Sounds like a right fine idea to me."

And moments later that's exactly what they were doing. Riding hell for leather away from Pickaxe. Around the corner of the hotel and out past the remaining buildings at this end of town. On into the gloom of descending night with the crackle of flames and gunfire fading rapidly behind them...

CHAPTER TWENTY-TWO

"WELL THIS HAS TURNED OUT TO BE ONE HELL OF A night!" raged Lobo Hines as he paced furiously back and forth across the plush carpeting of his private suite. Every time he turned to reverse course, he slammed his right fist into the palm of his left hand. "Blood in the street, men dead and wounded...My hotel shot up and set ablaze...The choking stink of that smoke is driving me nuts, by the way—somebody open a goddamned window!"

"Don't you think," Sarina Lopez said calmly from where she sat on an overstuffed divan, "that might allow in even more smoke from outside?"

"I don't care. There's bound to be a breath or two of fresh air with it. Open that window, like I said!" The agitated gesture accompanying this command sent Kelson scurrying to comply.

Lobo resumed pacing, kicking it off with another fist to palm smack. "How hard should it be," he wailed, "for a pack of so-called gun toughs to run down a lousy horse thief and some floozy riding with him?"

"She turned out to be more than just a floozy, Boss," Kelson protested. "She was packin' guns, too—and she knew how to use 'em!"

"That's sure different from how she acted when her and McGantry joined us out on the trail," spoke up Hilary Banks, who, along with Mel Dekker, was also present in the room.

"I know. She didn't show no signs of anything like that back at the Milestone farm, neither," agreed Kelson. "But it was a lot different story out front a little while ago. She was a doggone wildcat! That's part of what caught us so much by surprise."

"What's your excuse for the horse thief?" jeered Dekker. "You went after him *knowing* he showed signs of having some bark. Did he surprise you, too?"

Kelson's eyes narrowed. "Way it was, we had him —*and* the floozy—right where we wanted 'em. What really busted everything apart was that crazy shotgunner gallopin' outta nowhere up behind us."

"Somebody you were unable to identify," Dekker said pointedly.

"I'll tell you what I *can* identify," growled Kelson. "I can identify how he blew Sam Strong Eyes into chopped liver with one barrel of his blaster and how he damn near took my head off with the other. Then the whole street turned into a shootin' gallery with McGantry and his floozy—joined by a couple ragged-assed cowboys who also came outta nowhere—blazin' away partly at me and Dozier and partly tradin' lead with some fellas inside the barroom...While the maniac on horseback had switched to tryin' to trample me or split my skull open with swipes from his shotgun barrel.

"Me and Dozier finally made it to cover, but not before I put a bullet in that sumbitch on the horse. If he ain't dead already, I plan on followin' his blood trail come first light and finishin' the job before the sun sets again. With any luck, we'll have the rest swingin' from hang nooses within the same span of time."

"By luck or whatever means," said Lobo, "you'd better be able to back that up. I'll give you one more chance. I won't accept another failure!"

"I don't intend to come up short again. You can count on me, Boss."

Lobo grimaced. "But that still leaves the even bigger problem with those useless damn rifles. Thanks to you two"—scowling in the direction of Dekker and Hilary—"the condition they're in now makes them of no value to Toneka except as decorations for his tee-pee or maybe to use as war clubs."

"That's not fair," protested Hilary. "How was I supposed to suspect that preacher had such a sneaky side to him or that he even knew enough about guns to mess them up."

"You should have kept an eye on him at all times!" Dekker hissed.

"Yeah, and you should have not bashed his brains in with that damn rifle butt the way you did! If you hadn't," Lobo said in a tight voice, "then he wouldn't still be out cold, laying on a cot in Doc Gaines' treatment room looking like his next stop might be a slab at the undertaker's."

"I say he's faking it. I didn't hit him that stinkin' hard," Dekker insisted.

"The doc says different."

Dekker snorted. "That quack. For all we know, he might be in on it. Let me have a couple minutes alone with Hightower. I'll not only slap him out of his phony unconsciousness, next I'll show everybody some tricks that'll have him blabbing in no time where he hid those firing pins."

"I have no basis to question Dekker's persuasive skills," Sarina remarked dryly. "But Dr. Gaines has proven time and again he is no quack and he supports this community without taking sides. If his advice is that the minister's condition is too delicate to tamper with, then I would strongly advise listening to him."

"Sarina's right," Lobo said quickly and firmly. "We're going to go by what the doc says. He claims Hightower has what he calls a concussion and his brain is swollen from the force of the blow. If he rests undisturbed, the swelling will go down in a day or so—maybe as soon as tomorrow—and he should then wake up. So we wait."

"Yeah, but how much longer will Toneka wait?" Dekker wondered.

"Like the rest of us...as long as he has to," Lobo answered. "Now. There's nothing more we can do by staying here jawing. I say we all need to get some rest and I, for one, need to find a way to get that damn smoke stink out of my nostrils.

"Burt, I want two reliable men stationed at the doctor's place around the clock. They're not to interfere in any way with the doc's work, just make sure nobody but him messes with Hightower...First thing in the morning, take the men you need and go run down that horse thieving bastard and the rest. Check in with me before you head out."

With that, the Gun Wolf boss gave a dismissive wave of his hand. "All right, everybody beat it. Everybody but Sarina...Call it a night. Let's hope to hell things take a better turn tomorrow."

CHAPTER TWENTY-THREE

Letty Walburn leaned back from the task she'd been intently focused on for the nearly the past hour. Some of the tension relaxed out of her bony shoulders and she expelled a weary breath, aiming it upward from the corner of her mouth to push away a ringlet of sweat-damp hair trailing down above one eye. "There. That's about the best I can do," she announced. "The shoulder wound wasn't too bad, mostly just torn meat and muscle. The bullet's out of his side and I got the bleeding stopped. At least on the outside. He lost a lot of blood already, though, and he may be tore up on the inside, maybe still leaking in there...He needs a doctor, a real one, who knows more than me."

As Letty reached over to rinse her blood smeared hands in the pan of warm water her son Lee held out for her, the others gathered in the small, tidy kitchen of the Walburn home looked on in somber silence. Standing directly behind where his wife sat in a straight-backed wooden chair with their son kneeling on her left with the wash pan, was Fred Walburn.

Bunched near on Letty's right were the others—Lone, Velda, and the two cowboys from the Gold Tip fracas. Fred, Lone, and the older of the cowboys all held brightly burning lanterns high and steady to illuminate the tense work the woman had been performing. The subject of her ministrations was Billy Doyle, laid out on a blood-stained sheet that had been spread over the kitchen table. At the moment he was unconscious, his shirt was pulled wide open to expose the bullet wound he'd taken on his right side halfway between hip bone and rib cage.

Speaking into the quiet, Lone said, "He have a chance of makin' it?"

Letty hesitated before replying, "I think. But not without a doctor."

"Is there one in Pickaxe?" Velda asked.

Fred Walburn nodded. "There is. Doc Gaines."

"But, like everybody else," Lone said sourly, "on the payroll or under the thumb of Lobo Hines, I suppose."

"Actually, no," Walburn responded. "Gaines is not only a good doctor but he's also his own man. Lobo knows it's best for him to have a doctor in town so he cuts Gaines more slack than most. He also knows the doc ain't going nowhere on account of he has a bedridden wife at home who can't travel. So they're sort of stuck with each other, the doc and Lobo. Lobo gives him pretty much free rein and Gaines lives up to his oath to treat those in need—meaning owlhoot and decent folk alike."

"That's interesting, but kind of a moot point, isn't it?" questioned Velda. "I mean, taking the kid back into town with that wound is bound to draw attention—the kind that wouldn't take long for somebody to suspect how he got it. Plus, if you ask me it don't look like he's in shape for a ride back to town anyway."

"Absolutely not," said Letty, who'd risen from her tableside chair and was now starting to tend to the cuts and bruises and obviously broken nose of the younger cowboy. "Put this boy on a horse or even in the bed of a bouncing wagon to go that far, you'll surely start the bleeding again and what you'll end up delivering to the doc may already be a corpse."

That brought on more somber silence.

Until young Lee said, "Then why not bring Dr. Gaines out here?"

Lone's eyebrows lifted. "There's a chance for that? He goes out of town on house calls, does he?"

"Well, yeah," Walburn answered. "Doc comes out fairly regular to where somebody's reported bad sick or injured, even to deliver a baby now and then. Like I told you, Lobo trusts him on account of his sick wife at home."

"We'd have to give him a different reason than a gunshot wound," Velda said. "After the ruckus we raised before we lit out, Lobo's going to have eyes and ears on alert all over town. Any of 'em catch wind the doc is being called out on account of a shooting, it'll raise an alarm same as what I said before. They won't be taking no chances. Tomorrow you can be sure Lobo will be sending some men out after us, but that don't mean he wouldn't jump at a sooner chance if he smells one."

"I can tell the doc that pa got gored by a bull or some like, and ma can't get the bleeding stopped," suggested Lee.

"You? Who says you're the one going to tell anybody anything?" his father demanded to know.

"I'm the best choice, Pa. I can be convincing and I'd be least likely to draw suspicion. Besides, none of them" —he made a gesture to indicate Lone and the others— "can risk going back into town. I'm the best choice, I tell you."

"Now hold on a minute, son," said Lone, frowning. "You're makin' brave talk and you've got it thought out pretty smart. But there'd still be a fair amount of risk involved, even for you. Not only that, if anything went sour for you it would also rope in your ma and pa. We've already put your family in enough jeopardy by comin' here in the first place."

"You leave us worry about that," Letty declared. "The Doyles have been our neighbors for a good many years, we've seen Billy grow up from a toddler. You said yourself it was him led you here."

"Yeah, and that much was reasonable," Lone allowed. "He explained your place was closer than his and even he recognized how bad he needed some care. Plus, it was uncertain whether or not his stunt back in town got him recognized. In case it did and Kelson or somebody gave chase right away, they'd be bound to go straight to his folks' place and he didn't want to get caught laid up there."

Walburn grimaced. "Won't do his folks much good, not if Billy got recognized. Any Gun Wolves show up they'll be slow to believe the Doyles don't know anything. Be grounds for somebody getting leaned on mighty hard, regardless."

"Then maybe," Lee said with a display of jut-jawed firmness, "it would also be grounds for poking another stick into what Billy was trying to stir up with the things he had to say at the Milestone funeral. Maybe it would be enough to make his pa and some others decide they're sick of just stranding still and getting leaned on by Lobo's curs whenever their back hair get ruffled."

"That kind of talk—and the foolhardy action he coupled with it—is what put Billy in the condition you see before you." Fred Walburn's forehead puckered with torment. "How many additional friends and neighbors you think you'd see sprawled out the same way or worse if more tried following Billy's lead?"

Quietly, his son answered, "I don't know, Pa. But I'm beginning to see there are different ways a body can end up sprawled out. It might happen sudden from a position of standing tall...or get dragged out slower by first spending time on your knees."

CHAPTER TWENTY-FOUR

DR. BRODERICK GAINES WAS A BIG, PONDEROUS BULL OF A man crowding fifty. The fabric of the checkered shirt he wore under a voluminous frock coat that he'd peeled off shortly after entering the Walburn home was strained to the limit by his massive shoulders and stomach. His forearms, as revealed by the rolled up sleeves of the shirt, were beefy and hairless, his fingers stubby though nimble. The beard stubble on his heavy jowls was gray-flecked, as were his bushy eyebrows and the strands of thinning hair combed straight back atop his head. He had bright, intelligent eyes, a sausage nose, and a small, oddly delicate mouth squeezed between fleshy cheeks. However, there was nothing small or delicate about the voice that rumbled from that mouth when he spoke.

"Letty," he proclaimed, leaning back in the same wooden chair the woman herself had occupied just short of three hours earlier, "you did a mighty fine job on this wound. Wasn't really much left for me to do except close up some of the tearing on the inside before sewing him shut again. In fact, you get much better at treating hurts and ailments I might name you my junior partner so's you can handle these middle of the night calls and I can stay in bed once I get settled there."

Letty chuffed. "Looks to me, Brod Gaines, like you oughta concern yourself with getting out and about more, not less. You get any wider, you rascal, you'll have to trade your buggy for a freight wagon to haul you on these out of town calls."

The doctor chuckled. "True enough, Letty. But Pilar, the old gal who helps look after my wife is just too danged good a cook. I can't help taking second helpings of the meal she prepares."

"Well, as long as she takes good care of Estelle, I guess that's the main thing."

"She does that, to be sure." Wiping his hands on a damp towel, Gaines then said, "As to the further care of young Doyle here, the wounds are clean and the bleeding is stopped both inside and out. The only thing left is to keep any infection from setting in and keep him still so he has time to heal."

"Once he wakes up, keeping him still might be the hardest thing," said Letty. "As you can see and likely have heard, Billy has turned into quite the rambunctious young man." Then, with a sidelong glance toward her son, she added, "Him, and some others who show signs of it rubbing off on them as well."

Lee Walburn had won his argument for being the one to go into town and fetch the doctor. The only proviso had been that Lone and Velda accompanied him as far as the city limits where they held back, remaining out of sight but close and ready to ride in and be of aid in case anything went sour. Fortunately, Lee's fabricated story had been convincing enough to get a prompt response out of Gaines without raising any undue suspicion from the two Gun Wolves standing guard over the unconscious Hightower. Once Lee and the doc were clear of town, Lone and Velda made their presence known and the truth of the medical emergency was revealed. This not only did nothing to deter Gaines' willingness to proceed but actually seemed to hasten him a bit more.

In response now to Letty's remark about Billy Doyle's "rambunctious" turn and how it showed signs of spreading, the doctor's lips pooched out thoughtfully. "I have for some time wondered how long it would be before such a strain might start to show," he said. "Further, I have wondered if such a thing should be looked upon as a development to be welcomed...or something to be dreaded and discouraged."

Letty looked confused. "I – I'm not sure what you mean."

"I think I do," spoke up Lone, who, as before, had been crowded up close along with Lee and the older cowboy with lanterns held high to illuminate the work Gaines was performing on Billy's wound. "I think the doc is saying that good people showin' signs of pushin' back against the abuse of crud like Lobo Hines and his Gun Wolves is something to be cheered; but, at the same time, the cost of that kind of pushin' back is often high and bloody. What it comes down to in the end is pretty much what your son said a few hours back...A body needin' to make up their mind whether they want to live life standin' tall—or on their knees."

"Saying it like that makes it sound like the swell of a revolution or some such," said Letty, her face switching from a look of confusion to a troubled scowl.

"I don't know that it's anything on a scale quite that grand. Nobody's looking to overthrow a government," Gaines told her.

Letty aimed her scowl directly at him. "Whatever you call it, you sound as if you're inclined to be supportive of it. You, a man of medicine, a healer. You heard McGantry. The cost is bound to be high and bloody."

"Isn't it already that?" responded Gaines, forming his own scowl. "And didn't you hear me say I'm torn between welcoming and dreading what's sure to result from common, decent men attempting to resist a force like the Gun Wolves? Yet there's no getting around the fact that Lobo Hines has had Pickaxe and the whole surrounding area in his grip for too long now and there's no sign of him easing up on how hard he means to keep squeezing. If anything, it's growing steadily tighter and more vicious. You don't have to look any farther than the murder of Henry and Belle Milestone for proof of that."

"And the kidnapping of their daughters," Lee was quick to add.

"That hasn't been established for certain yet," his mother countered, though not with much conviction.

"Yeah, it has, Ma," said Lee. "I didn't say anything before—though I see where I probably should have—but I went back to the Milestone place with Billy this afternoon. Well, yesterday afternoon I guess you'd call it now. Anyway, it was time enough for the ashes to cool to the point we were able to dig thoroughly through 'em... There was nothing there that gave any sign the girls got caught in the fire. But that didn't make them any less gone and all it left was one explanation for how and where they went."

"Is that when Billy made up his mind to go chargin' into town after Kelson and Lobo?" Lone wanted to know.

Lee hung his head. "He went a little crazy, yeah. He vowed how he was gonna do all kinds of things. I - I didn't really think he would. At least not right away and not all by himself."

"Your father is over at the Doyles now, telling them what happened." Letty sounded suddenly exhausted. "He wanted to warn them to be on guard in case Billy was recognized and some of Lobo's men show up looking for him. We know now at least that part isn't a worry. He also was going to try and discourage them from coming here and risk getting caught in what might transpire in case Billy's trail is able to be followed come daylight. But I don't know if he'll have any success keeping them away. Fred should be back pretty soon, I expect we'll find out then."

"As far as anybody following Billy's trail come daybreak," said Velda, who had been standing by mostly quiet ever since returning with the doctor, "now seems like as good a time as any for me and McGantry to share with the rest of you some thoughts we had on that likelihood."

All eyes swung to her and waited to hear more.

"Way we figure," Velda continued, beginning to relate a plan she and Lone had roughed out while waiting on the outskirts of Pickaxe for Lee to go in and roust the doctor, "is that there's no way in blazes somebody like Lobo won't be sending men, probably a small army, to get some hard payback for the way we tore up his town and especially his hotel. What Billy did was just part of it, remember. The whole lot of us—me, McGantry, Reese, Dutton, *and* Billy—combined to cut a swath Lobo will feel compelled to seek revenge on each and every one of us for."

The "Reese" and "Dutton" Velda spoke of by name were Bud Reese and Jeff Dutton, the two cowboys who'd tangled with the Gold Tip bouncers and then made the choice to jump in deeper by taking Velda's side when lead started flying. Reese was the older of the pair; Dutton the younger one who'd gotten the brunt of the physical working over from the barroom bruisers. When they finally got the opening to introduce themselves fully, they revealed they had recently completed a three-year stint with a cattle ranch up in Montana and, not wanting to face another Montana winter, were on the drift southward to eventually hook up with a new outfit in the more reasonable climes of southern Colorado or maybe New Mexico.

"Since McGantry and I both know a little something about tracking and running down hombres," Velda went on, "we also know that it can be a two-way street. Meaning, you can only chase a critter for as long as it keeps running. If you're skilled enough and have a little luck, you catch up on your terms. But you've always got to watch out for the chance a critter will get sick of running and turn back on you...That's when things might go from being the hunter to becoming the hunted."

When she hesitated for a moment to let that much sink in, Reese said, "Let me guess. You and McGantry ain't the types who plan on runnin' much at all before settin' your course as hunters of those comin' to hunt you."

Lone smiled. "You catch on quick."

"Fought in a few runnin' skirmishes durin' the war. Over a period of days it was like a see-saw as far as who was chargin' and who was fallin' back."

Lifting his brows above eyes that darted back and forth between Lone and Velda, Dr. Gaines said, "You mean you actually intend to head out in the morning to purposely confront whatever force Lobo sends?"

"Not necessarily confront 'em in a head-to-head way like you imply," replied Lone, his smile falling into a crooked grin. "But we'll quick let 'em know they've smacked up against something that not only ain't runnin' but is gonna make it damn costly for anybody to keep comin' after us."

"Not to sound discouraging, but may I ask why?" pressed the medic. "What stake do you have in this that would cause you to take such action?"

"McGantry and I came here for reasons of our own, but ones that were almost certain to put us at odds with Lobo's operation," Vela explained. "The timing of our showing up happening in conjunction with anything else is strictly coincidence. But that doesn't mean these other things we've now seen and heard about are matters easily shrugged off. If doing what we came prepared to do anyway turns out to be beneficial to others, then so be it."

"The enemy of my enemy is my friend," muttered Gaines.

Letty gave him a look. "There you go again, saying stuff that only half makes sense."

Before the doctor could say anything further, the

sound of hoofbeats approaching outside became discernible to all.

Quickly reaching to turn down the wick on the lantern he was still holding, Lone said to Lee and Reese, "Lower your lights. Everybody stand clear of the windows."

"It's only my husband returning," Letty assured everyone.

"Maybe so," Lone replied crisply. "But it won't hurt to be careful until we're sure."

CHAPTER TWENTY-FIVE

"WELL, I GOT WORD TO THE DOYLES ABOUT THEIR BOY, and I warned 'em to be on the lookout in case any Gun Wolves came around snooping for him. Got them to hold off rushing over here, too, at least not right away... But what I'm fixing to pass on now, what I found out in return whilst I was at the Doyles, plumb jumps to the head of the line as far as importance and big-time concern for just about everybody."

These were the words that began pouring excitedly out of a harried-looking Fred Walburn the minute he shoved through the front door of his home and came marching into the kitchen where everyone was gathered. The sight of Billy still stretched unconscious atop the table checked Walburn down some but his expression remained anxious, as did the restless shifting of his feet even after he'd stopped moving forward.

"For Heaven' sake, keep your voice down," his wife chided him. "But then, once you've managed that, don't leave us dangling—get on with the telling of whatever this great new concern is. What else has happened?"

Walburn grimaced. "Nothing yet. But if Lobo Hines's latest scheme pans out, this whole territory is going to be in for hellation and bloodletting like nobody's seen in near two decades!"

"Blast it, man, get on with it," said Dr. Gaines. "What are you talking about?"

"Okay, okay. It's got me a little rattled, I don't mind saying." Walburn hitched up a wooden chair and sat down on it backwards, folding his arms across the top. "Pour me a cup of coffee, will you, Letty, and I'll tell you all what you ain't going to like the sound of. I got it from Noah Felton, who was at the Doyles when I arrived."

"At this time of night?" said his wife, holding out the requested cup of coffee.

"That's right. For old Noah to be out traipsing near midnight, you know it's got to be something plenty important. He had with him his hired man, that colored fella Ralston. And also Ralston's nephew Hiram, who works in town at Wilkes' livery. It was Hiram who overhead some things that worried him enough to come high-tailing out to tell his uncle and then, at his uncle's insistence, old Noah."

"Must've been awfully convincing to cause Noah not to wait until morning to pass it along," noted Letty.

Gaines nodded. "Hiram is a good, honest, hard-working lad. I wouldn't have any trouble taking his word on most anything."

"Yeah, I've always heard the same. Likewise for Ralston. Though this is a time I wish they were better known as tall tale spinners." Walburn paused to take a drink of his coffee. "It all started, surprisingly enough, with that preacher, Hightower, most of us here met earlier today when he was on hand to speak at the burial of Henry and Belle Milestone. We all knew him and his daughter was headed into Pickaxe afterwards. I believe you and Miss Velda rode on in with them, didn't you, McGantry?"

"That's right," said Lone. "We left 'em at the livery you spoke of, where the boy Hiram works. We were fixin' to also board our horses there, but then things took a different turn and we didn't."

"Uh-huh. Hiram mentioned something about that too, about how there was a dispute when you found a horse in the corral out back that you claimed had been stolen from you. But that" —a dismissive wave of Walbun's hand— "is of no concern to this other matter. After you parted ways with the Hightowers, you see, it apparently didn't take long before a whole lot of things took some other turns. It started with the arrival of Lobo Hines and several others. A few, including Burt Kelson, broke off to go after the stolen horse. Lobo and the rest showed more interest in the Hightowers and their wagon that was parked in a lot out by the side corrals. Wilkes, the livery operator, was ordered to stay out of the way. But Hiram got unexpectedly caught pumping water into a horse trough out near the wagon. Because he hid in the shadows to keep from being spotted and getting in trouble, he ended up seeing and overhearing everything that took place."

"What possible interest did Lobo have in the Hightowers?" Velda wanted to know. "Was he bent on running them out of town before they ever got the chance to hold even a single service?"

"No, Lobo's interest in Hightower had nothing to do with his preachifying. What he wanted was the cargo being hauled in that wagon."

Lone scowled. "What cargo? The boxes of Bibles?"

"Not hardly," Walburn said somewhat smugly. "What Lobo was waiting for was the crates of late model Winchester repeating rifles."

"Wait a minute. You saying Hightower and his daughter are gunrunners?" Velda asked, her tone incredulous.

Walburn shook his head. "Not willingly. Not from what Hiram was able to make of it. Leastways that was the case for the reverend. But not so the girl, who turns out to not really be his daughter at all. As soon as Lobo and his bunch showed up, she ran to one of 'em—that Dekker character who arrived in town a while back and got in so thick with the boss Wolf—and commenced hugging and kissing on him like he was the long lost love of her life."

"This is all sounding crazier by the minute," declared Velda. "We rode and camped with those people for days. I never—"

Lone cut her off by abruptly saying, "The weight of the wagon! Don't you remember how uncommonly heavy it was when we near busted a gut pryin' it up to put the wheel back on and get it out of the creek bed ahead of that storm? And the bed inside, when we crawled in under the canopy to ride out the storm, was oddly high. A false bottom, it sounds like now. I should have put some of those things together and recognized there was something mighty fishy right then and there—how they had to be haulin' something besides just Bibles."

"Okay. I guess maybe I can accept about the guns," Velda allowed grudgingly. "But to also believe Hope was just masquerading as the reverend's daughter?"

"As I hear these pieces being laid out," said Dr. Gaines, "I think I might be able to fit some of them together in a way to help explain the whole picture. That doesn't mean it will make a picture that's any prettier, mind you, but I can't help that.

"It starts with my awareness of the fact there is a young lady being held against her will, under the watch of Sarina Lopez, at the Gold Tip Hotel. I was summoned to care for her a little under three weeks ago. She was frightened into a near catatonic state. Not eating or drinking, not responding to kindness or threats, either one."

"What was frightening her so badly?"

"Fear of the unknown, of being torn away from everything she knew and felt comfortable with after leading a previously very sheltered life. And also the fear that her father might be in equal or worse danger while her captivity was being used by some bad people to force him to do something he didn't want to do. Her words. I learned these things," Gaines explained, "in the course of several lengthy sessions with the girl—who said her name was Hope, by the way—during which I finally got her to take some nourishment and open up a bit."

Lone said, "You're thinkin' this girl is the real Hope, the genuine daughter of Reverend Hightower?"

"So it would seem," Gaines replied. "I didn't get many details from her beyond what I just stated. But combined with what Hiram saw and overheard—the gun cargo being hidden against the will of a traveling minister, the 'daughter' traveling with him turning out to be a phony replacement—it all seems to fit that the girl Sarina is holding was being used as leverage to get Hightower to transport the rifles."

"Rifles no doubt stolen. Probably from a military armory somewhere," surmised Velda. "Pretty damn clever, actually, to move them under the noses of what must have been a massive search operation by hiding them the last place anybody would ever think to look."

"Clever maybe. But it didn't go without a hitch," Walburn said. "This is again according to Hiram. When it came time to unload the guns it turned out the preacher had rigged them in some way—Hiram wasn't clear exactly how—so they wouldn't fire. Then he refused to fix whatever he'd done until his real daughter was safely returned to him."

Lone smiled. "Guess the old boy ain't strictly a 'turn the other cheek' type. But I don't reckon pullin' a stunt like that went over very good with Lobo."

"Not only Lobo," Walburn grunted, "but even worse with Dekker. He got so mad he took one of the rifles and gave the preacher such a whack on the head he knocked him cold."

"He sure did. He gave Hightower a concussion that, as of a couple hours ago, rendered him still unconscious," related Dr. Gaines. When all eyes swung his way once again, he went on, "They sent for me after Dekker did his damage. I had the reverend brought to my treatment room where I left him resting comfortably when I came here as summoned by Lee."

"That explains those two Gun Wolf skunks who were hanging around outside your office," remarked Lee.

"That's right. They're on hand to report to Lobo any sign of Hightower coming around."

"Will he come around? Do you expect the reverend to be okay if and when he does regain consciousness?" asked Velda.

"I suspect so," Gaines answered. "Head injuries can be tricky, though. But as long as Hightower hasn't had any prior serious concussion, he'll most likely be okay."

"Not as okay as he is for however long as he stays knocked cold," pointed out Lone. "If he wakes up, a very angry Lobo is gonna want some answers out of him and he won't be gentle about goin' after 'em...And I mean un-gentle in ways that will make a rifle butt to the head look like a love tap."

"Uh-huh. That could be bad news for the preacher," said Walburn with a grim twist to his mouth. "But that ain't the worst news. I still haven't got to that part. You see, if Lobo gets those rifles in working order his plan is to sell them for a high mark-up payable in gold...to a wild-eyed Injun renegade by the name of Toneka!"

"Toneka," muttered Lone in distaste. "I've heard rumblings about him. He's a hotblood Sioux pup who's been tryin' to stir up trouble on the rez for three or four years now. If he all of a sudden got his hands on a haul of Winchester repeaters he'd have little or no trouble findin' followers to join him on a sweep of bloody raids."

Walburn looked at his wife. "Do you see now, Letty, why news of this possibility was enough to bring Noah Felton out in the middle of the night?" Then, his expression turning even more grave, his gaze shifted to his son. "And you, you and Billy and others who've been pushing for us outlying farmers and ranchers to take more of a stand against Lobo and his Gun Wolves? It looks like you've got you wish. If we don't rise up and stop Lobo from going ahead with this, six dozen

Winchesters in the hands of Sioux renegades would mean slaughter and ravaging like nobody ever wanted to see again. Yeah, the army would show up and quell such an uprising eventually...But not before most of us and everything we've worked for would be wiped out in ways more terrible than you can imagine. So, throughout the night, Felton and Doyle will be spreading the word for a gathering to be held here tomorrow noon. From there, we'll make a plan to try and stave off our slaughter."

CHAPTER TWENTY-SIX

"WELL. WE SURE LANDED SMACK IN THE THICK OF SOME stuff, didn't we?" said Velda, leaning back on the front porch bench where she was seated and tipping her head against the outer wall of the Walburn house. The night was still, the air moderately cool, just short of turning expelled breaths into visible vapor. Some long, stringy clouds were momentarily blotting out the moon but a spray of bright stars was still pouring bluish silver illumination down onto the crests of the surrounding hills.

Sitting splay-legged on the porch floor at one end of the bench, Lone replied, "I got no argument for that. We didn't figure on waltzin' in and out of here without steppin' on some toes—but there's sure more feet stompin' back from more directions than we expected."

"Although," said Velda, "you sorta have the right to look at it as your toes—and, more to the point, your horse's hooves—being in the clear. After all, your purpose for coming here was to reclaim Ironsides. You've accomplished that. So you don't really have a reason not to ride out and continue your journey back to Fort Collins. It's not like you owe anybody around here anything, least of all sticking out your neck to fight the Gun Wolves on behalf of those who've groveled all this time instead of making the fight sooner on their own."

Lone chuffed. "If I believed you really thought that of me, I'd put a boot in that pretty hind end of yours. We've only ridden together a few days, but I know you're savvy enough to have read me better than that. I strike up a partnership with somebody, even a temporary one, I hold up my end until the job is done. So yeah, I got my horse. But you ain't got your man Mitchum yet, and the job ain't done until you do."

"What if I'm beginning to think he ain't worth the risk of wading through Lobo's whole Gun Wolf army?"

"If you said it and meant it, I'd honor that as your call to make." Lone turned his head and eyed Velda shrewdly. "But I ain't ready to buy you thinkin' that way. I've seen the fire in your eyes too many times when you speak of takin' Mitchum down. And I also recall what you said inside a little while ago about how the things we've seen and heard since we got here ain't easily shrugged off...Meanin' you recognize, like I do, there are more reasons to take a cut at the Gun Wolves than just for the sake of gettin' to Mitchum."

This was the first opportunity Lone and Velda had had to talk alone together since their palaver on the edge of Pickaxe waiting for Lee Walburn to go in and fetch the doctor. So much more had been revealed in the handful of hours since then. And with the possibility of a renegade Indian uprising being triggered (literally, given the availability of Winchester repeating rifles looming as the catalyst), so much more was at stake.

"You're right on all counts," Velda admitted in response to Lone's observations. "But if you're so keen on remembering things I said, then you should also recall what I said about those kidnapped Milestone sisters. How desperately I want to see them rescued."

When Lone gave a nod, she continued. "Well, that's something I truly would trade for Mitchum. If, amidst all that is about to break loose, there was a way we could find those girls and save them, I wouldn't care if it meant allowing Mitchum to get away."

"Not that I'm against it but tryin' to save those girls is a pretty tall order," Lone said. "We don't even know where to start lookin' for—"

"Oh, but I think we do," Velda interrupted. "When Doc Gaines spoke of the real Hope Hightower being held captive at the Gold Tip, he mentioned a woman named Sarina Lopez. We also heard that name from Wilkes, the fella at the livery stable, who said Sarina handles the 'entertainment end of things' for Lobo. Don't seem like much of a stretch to figure that somebody who'd hold a girl captive for one reason—namely, to leverage the girl's father—would be above holding other girls captive as well. Fresh young girls who've been kidnapped for the purpose of turning them into 'entertainment' for Lobo's special guests and then, eventually, after they've been used and starting to show too much wear, handing 'em on down to the crib trade."

Lone cocked a brow. "Anybody ever tell you you got a real nasty outlook on human nature?"

"Comes with the territory. But does it make me wrong?"

"No, I'm afraid it don't. What's more," Lone added, "payin' a return visit to the Gold Tip to look for the Milestone sisters also fits with the other gal you just mentioned, the real Hope. We know for sure she's there so we oughta try to get her out too. She's only safe as long as Doc Gaines does his part to keep her father conked out. But sooner or later, if she's as pretty as the phony Hope, you can bet there are plans to use her for some 'entertainment' as well."

Velda's face took on an expression of disgust. "That kind of treatment by men is loathsome enough though, no offense, not surprising. But hearing another woman involved in it is even worse. Was I to think about it, and it wouldn't have to be very hard, it just might be that another trade I'd be willing to make for Mitchum would be if it meant a chance to put a bullet in Sarina Lopez."

"Don't give up," Lone told her. "If we end up havin' to shoot our way back into the Gold Tip, maybe you'll get your chance to ventilate both."

Now it was Velda's turn to arch a brow. "I didn't know you had it in you, McGantry, but by golly you know how to sweet talk a gal...and I don't mean that remark about my pretty hind end."

Lone was glad for the deep shadows cast by the porch overhang; he might have blushed a little.

Just then the front door opened and Reese and Dutton stepped out.

"Mrs. Walburn is wantin' to know if she should lay out some sleepin' pallets inside," said Reese. "Are you two figurin' on gettin' some shuteye before we head out?"

Lone squinted up at him. "'We'?"

Reese set his mouth and gave a curt nod. "That's

right. Me and Dut had a chance to talk it over after the doctor left a while ago, and we decided we're of a mind to toss in with you when you go to 'front those Gun Wolf hombres you figure to come ridin' out at first light. If you'll have us, that is. We don't pretend to be gun sharps or any such like, but we've been in a scrape or two. And since we hotfooted off without our own horses, Mr. Walburn said he'd borrow us a couple of his to use."

Lone and Velda exchanged looks. "Well now. We're obliged for the offer. We could sure use a couple more guns," Lone said. "But, for starters, are you sure you're up to it, Dutton? No offense, but you took a whale of a beatin' from those two oxen back at the hotel."

Dutton, both eyes starting to blacken and his busted nose stuffed with cotton, gave a firm nod. "I've been tore up worse than this by rank bulls and bucking broncs, I can handle it."

Lone grinned. "I believe you. But are you fellas clear on the whole of what you're steppin' in to? You got a taste of it in town last night, but that was just a handful of Lobo's Wolves caught pretty much off guard. What we expect he'll be sendin' out come morning will be ten or a dozen hardcases on a blood scent aimin' to spill plenty more. They—and no doubt with Lobo whippin' 'em up—will see last night as an embarrassment they'll want real bad to get payback for."

Dutton nodded again. "Like the doc said earlier, it ain't a pretty picture. But we're clear on what it paints. Not only what it might mean to face this first batch of hardcases, but the rest of it, too...How these good, honest, hard-workin' folks have been bullied and shoved around by Lobo and his gunnies. Murdered over pigs, for God's sake. And their womenfolk stole away. It plumb ain't right!"

"Fellas like Dut and me don't amount to a whole lot," Reese said. "We work, we drift, we work some more. We don't do no particular harm, but we don't make no particular mark neither. The closest I ever came was in the war. But even then I was just another scared, skinny kid runnin' whichever way some officer told me to go and hopin' I didn't get my head blowed off followin' his orders.

"But this. What's shapin' up here amounts to something. With you two leadin' the way and Walburn and his neighbors ready to finally band together an make a move against Lobo and his bloody plans...Well, like I said, it amounts to something. And bein' part of it means a chance for a body to amount to something, too. So for me and Dut to turn our backs and ride on, say it's none of our concern... No, we don't reckon that's what we want."

Velda smiled. "I think I'm safe in also speaking for McGantry when I say we're glad that's how you reckon and you're surely welcome to ride with us."

"Good. What do we tell Mrs. Walburn about the sleeping pallets?" Dutton asked.

"Tell her not to bother," said Lone. "It's less than three hours to daybreak. I'm thinkin' we oughta go ahead and move out, find us a good spot on the course we figure the Gun Wolves will be taking, and get set up. We can rest while we're waitin' for 'em to show."

Reese grunted. "Just like bein' in the army again. Always movin' out from some place comfortable to some place bound to be less comfortable."

CHAPTER TWENTY-SEVEN

THE MOON EMERGED FROM BEHIND ITS CLOUD COVERING as they rode away from the Walburn farm, providing decent visibility for their return toward Pickaxe. In keeping with what Lone and Velda had initially roughed out during their wait for Lee and the doctor, the plan was simple and straightforward: Catch the Gun Wolves in an unexpected ambush and wipe out as many as possible before they ever knew what hit them. This would not only turn back their intended pursuit but hopefully diminish a significant number of the force for what was now building as an overdue follow-up by the surrounding farmers and ranchers.

Having been on the wrong end of too many attempted ambushes, Lone was never totally at ease setting one himself. But the practical side of him knew there were times when that's what was called for. Current circumstances boiled down to the Gun Wolves being too formidable and too numerous to try going at head on. The only chance to come out on top of this initial confrontation and then, beyond that, to rescue the abducted girls and allow the farmers and ranchers to turn the tide against Lobo Hines once and for all, was to whittle down his superior force with small, quick, surprise slashes. How effective this morning's opening slash was, would go a long way toward the success of what was intended to follow.

About a mile short of Pickaxe, they came upon a spot laid out quite suitable for their plan. The trail out of town passed through a narrow cut between two rocky ridges choked along their bases on either side by brush and gnarled trees.

"Couldn't ask for much better," Lone declared, reining up and pausing to survey the scene spread out before them in the wash of moon- and starlight that was beginning to brighten with the creeping approach of pre-dawn.

"I don't disagree," said Reese. "But how can we be sure Lobo's men will come this way?"

"Because this is the way we came last night," answered Velda. "I remember passing through that cut. If the Gun Wolves are setting out to track us and they have somebody able to read sign even halfway decent, they could hardly miss sticking with our trail to this point."

"And let's not forget we're almost certain to have the element of surprise on our side," pointed out Lone. "The Gun Wolves are mean and tough, I won't dispute 'em that. But I'm willin' to bet that after all this time of havin' everybody cowed to do what they say without hardly no sass, they're also more than a little on the complacent side."

"Meanin' what, exactly?" said Dutton.

"Meanin' a more cautious and suspicious character

—like me, for instance—might approach that cut and think about the possibility of it bein' a good place for an ambush." Lone paused to let his mouth spread into a crooked grin. "But a pack of bullyin' scoundrels who are too used to havin' nobody ever buck back against 'em, I see them gallopin' in without any such worry enterin' their heads."

"Until," Reese said, copying Lone's grin, "we start enterin' in some .44 caliber worries when we commence blowin' their punkins clean off."

Lone's mouth pulled straight. "Yeah. That's the general idea."

"HOPE I didn't wake you up, Boss," said Burt Kelson when a tousle-haired Lobo answered the door to his suite in response to Kelson's knock.

"Not much worry about that," grumbled Lobo. "With that damn smoke stink bugging me all night I hardly got a wink. I might as well have let Milestone raise his blasted pigs and allowed their stink to waft into town, it couldn't have been much worse! I'm ordering a whitewashing crew to double coat the entire font of the hotel, starting first thing this morning. If that don't smother that rotten sink then I swear I'll burn down the whole goddamned joint and re-build it from scratch!"

Kelson shifted uncomfortably in the doorway. "Well, uh, I hope it don't come to that, Boss. The fresh coats of whitewash oughta do it. If not, it looks like there's a storm buildin' off to the northwest. That oughta help, too...uh, long as it don't sluice off the whitewash, that is."

"Let me worry about that," snapped Lobo. "You're here so early, I trust, because you're ready to start out after that horse-thieving bastard and his wildcat of a partner who started the fire in the first place. Is that it?"

"You bet. I've got ten of our best saddled and ready to head out. It's gettin' light enough for us to pick up their trail. I sure wish I had Sam Long Eyes to cut sign, but we got a fella named Tibbets who's pretty good. With the trail so fresh and them not likely to have gone very far in the dark, not knowin' the territory and all, we'll run 'em to ground alright. And if I wounded that shotgunnin' sumbitch like I think I did, that'll help, too."

"I don't care how you get it done, just do it," Lobo said with a scowl.

"By the way, I checked in at Doc Gaines on the way here," Kelson reported. "That preacher is still conked out but the doc is watchin' him real close. Says he still expects him to come out of it sooner or later."

Lobo's scowl deepened. "It better not be too damned much later or I might decide to let Dekker try his idea of bringing the holy man around. I've done everything I can to keep a lid on it, but if word somehow leaks out to Toneka that the rifles have arrived yet I haven't notified him, he's apt to come swooping off the rez after them."

"Be kinda dumb of him to try and make trouble without 'em, wouldn't it? You said yourself," Kelson reminded, "that him and his hotblood followers wouldn't stand much of a chance against us Gun Wolves."

"But I don't want to *fight* the red-skinned devil, not even in a sure victory," Lobo insisted. "I want to *deal* with the damn fool in an attempt to learn the source of his gold. If it turns into a fight and the idiot gets himself killed, where will that leave me?"

Kelson edged a half step back out of the doorway. "Don't worry, Boss. It'll work out. Me and the boys will go run down these troublemakers. I promise to try and bring you back one to hang. By the time we return, I bet that preacher will be up and about and you'll find a way to squeeze what you need to know out of him. Mark my words, it'll all work out."

Lobo smacked his right fist into his left palm. "It better...And it had better start pretty damned quick!"

CHAPTER TWENTY-EIGHT

"THERE'S THE SIGNAL. THEY'RE COMING," VELDA CALLED from her side of the cut.

"I see it," Lone replied from his side. "Let 'em come... That's what we're here for."

Dawn had arrived. The moon and stars and their inky backdrop had all faded to a pale gray canopy overhead. To the northwest, a cloud bank colored much darker gray was building ominously thicker and higher. Along the clear eastern horizon, though, a rose-gold glow was getting ready to give way to the first sliver of full sunlight.

Lone and Velda were positioned on what would be the exit end of the cut for anyone passing through from the direction of town. Lone was on the north side of the gap, kneeling on a rocky shelf about ten feet off the ground; Velda was low on the south side, tucked into a vertical seam in the rocks, with a tangle of brush for added cover. Reese and Dutton were positioned similarly on either side at the cut's entrance.

The plan was to let the Gun Wolf riders enter the

cut and pass most of the way through before Lone and Velda opened up on them. Hitting this wall of lead would cause the Wolves who weren't immediately cut down to do one of two things—either scramble for what meager cover they could find or, more likely, try to turn and flee out of the cramped confines of the gap. Either way, Reese and Dutton would be waiting to slam the back door and then proceed to squeeze the would-be hunters between *two* walls of mercilessly ripping lead.

Once Reese sent the signal that riders were approaching, Lone slowly inhaled and expelled a deep breath, then willed himself into a pattern of steady, measured breathing. He shifted his weight slightly, tightened his grip on his Winchester Yellowboy and waited. The morning air was still, everything was quiet. The low rumble of approaching hoofbeats became discernible, gradually growing louder as they drew nearer. Lone couldn't resist leaning forward just a bit until he could look out the throat of the cut and see the dust boil of the oncoming pack.

Easing back, he traded glances with Velda. Her lovely, clear-eyed face was set in that calm, determined expression he'd become so familiar with and grown to admire.

The hoofbeats grew louder and closer. Apparently confident of the trail they were following, the riders were coming at a pretty good clip. Entering the narrow gap would slow them some—and shortly after that as many as possible were due to be slowed permanently.

When the pack came into full view of his vantage point, Lone immediately recognized the features of Burt Kelson riding in the lead. Lone and Velda had decided up front—for the sake of not duplicating shots on the same target—that he would take whoever came through the cut first and she would take the next in line. Had it been otherwise, Lone surely would have regretted not getting a crack at the Gun Wolf lieutenant. Fortunately, it wasn't something denied him. Plus, no matter how much additional damage this ambush might do, robbing Lobo of one of his key men would be a telling blow in and of itself.

So, with one squeeze of the Yellowboy's trigger, Lone struck that blow. Entering at a downward angle, the bullet hit just above Kelson's left ear and blew the right side of his head out in a spray of gore and bone fragments. He was knocked from his saddle and instantly trampled by the horse coming behind. The rider of that horse had no awareness of any of this, however, because a near simultaneous heart shot from Velda made him just as dead as Kelson and his body, too, fell under trampling hooves.

From there, the space within the walls of the cut turned into a wild scene of chaos and bloodshed. Horses screamed, men cursed, guns roared and bullets tore through flesh, muscle, bone, and sometimes hammered mercifully against nothing more than rocks. Blue powder smoke roiled and mixed with clouds of dust kicked up by the stamping, churning hooves of the panicked animals of the men being knocked off their backs. Lone kept jacking fresh rounds into his Yellowboy and then quickly firing them at bobbing heads and whirling bodies in the thickening haze below. He could hear the guns of Velda, Reese, and Dutton barking just as aggressively and, as a result, saw men jerking from bullet impacts and pitching to the ground.

As expected, some of the pack—totaling roughly a

dozen men, by Lone's estimate—wheeled their mounts and tried to retreat from the barrage poured into them by Lone and Velda. This only succeeded in rushing them to meet the hail of lead that Reese and Dutton had waiting.

A few of the Wolves got off some return fire, but all were futile displays of desperation lacking even a target to aim at. In the end, the only thing that saved any of them was the boiling clouds of dust and smoke that obscured things to a point where three were able to squirt frantically back out the way they'd entered. Even at that, though, two of those were sagging precariously in their saddles, indicating they'd hardly gotten away unscathed.

With the gunfire ceased and the rataplan of the fleeing riders fading away, Lone made his way down off the ledge, replacing spent cartridges in the Yellowboy as he did. Velda appeared, also reloading as she moved forward. Her eyes were narrowed and her expression had gone from determined to grim. A steak of dust ran across one cheek.

"There's a bloody piece of business done," she declared. "Not exactly a noble act perhaps, but at least the world is better off with fewer girl-stealing, murder-over-pigs pieces of human trash."

Lone understood she was justifying to herself the slaughter she had just participated in. All he could do was nod in agreement.

Reese and Dutton came walking toward them through the thinning smoke and dust haze, stepping over fallen bodies.

"Sorry we let some of the skunks get away," was the first thing out of Reese's mouth. It was accompanied by an earnestly sorrowful expression, one mirrored by Dutton. "Guess me and Dut are a little out of practice when it comes to throwin' lead that hot and heavy."

"You both did fine," Lone assured him. "We not only turned the tables on the force sent to run us down, we took out Lobo's top man in the process. I think it's safe to say we rattled hell out of the Wolf boss in a way he's long overdue for."

"Actually, in a cockeyed kind of way," said Velda, "by letting those three run off we will have begun rattling Lobo all the sooner and given him that much longer to fret and wonder just what is going on. If we'd have cut down everybody who rode after us, it would have taken hours for Lobo to realize something had gone wrong. The whole day could've passed and he would have felt confident thinking it was just taking that long for his mongrels to run us to ground. Now he's going to be left feeling anything *but* confident."

"I like the thought of that, the thought of the big, bad Gun Wolf boss doin' some squirming," stated Reese.

"I do too," agreed Dutton. "But him knowin' sooner about his pack gettin' chewed up like we done here, ain't that gonna put him on guard and end up makin' it harder for the farmers and ranchers who are plannin' to form up and make their move on him?"

"It'll put Lobo on guard, that's true," allowed Lone. "But he ain't gonna know for sure against who or what. If he believes, rightfully so, his men got bushwhacked by those they went after—namely us, a misfit bunch made up of a horse thief, a wildcat, and a couple rowdy cowboy drifters—he won't have any reason to think we'd be crazy enough to come back to town looking for more trouble. The main thing he'll have to wrestle with as far as we're concerned is whether or not he wants to risk sending out more men, which I suspect he can't really afford, for another try at getting revenge on us. No matter what he decides about that, none of it will give him any warning or cause to prepare for the farmers and ranchers."

Velda's forehead puckered. "Why do you say you don't think Lobo can afford to send out any more men?"

"Matter of numbers. I count eight we killed here," Lone said, gesturing to the bodies scattered across the floor of the gap. "Plus two of the three who rode away looked to me to have been wounded fairly bad. Add in the hombre Billy Doyle killed last night on the street and the one I wounded, it tallies up to nine dead and three left at less than a hundred percent. That's a pretty big bite out of Lobo's pack in less than twenty-four hours."

Velda pooched her lips thoughtfully. "I see what you mean. According to Doc Gaines and Walburn, Lobo has been running things with only about twenty full-time Gun Wolf enforcers."

"That means we whittled his army darn near in half!" exclaimed Reese.

"Not quite so fast," cautioned Velda. "Yeah, we've no doubt taken out a big bite, like McGantry said. But we can't forget the fugitives Lobo harbors as a big part of his operation. You got to reckon some of them would side with him, for their own sake, if he was under a big enough threat."

Lone said, "Yet even if there's, say, a dozen such—figurin' on the high end—that still means we've whittled what we're up against by a third or more. I call that a good morning's work."

"Never heard anybody say otherwise," Velda responded. "Thing now is for us to gather up all these guns and any other worthwhile gear and take it back to Walburn's place where the other farmers and ranchers are scheduled to be meeting. Let's hope they show up still of a mind to put it to good use."

"I think they will. I think the news Doyle and Felton went off to spread is the kick in the pants they've been needin'," said Lone. "But before we offer any of this booty to anybody else, I think Reese and Dutton are owed first dibs to replace the horses and gear they lost in town last night...So commence your choosin', fellas, then the sooner the better for us makin' dust the hell away from here."

CHAPTER TWENTY-NINE

Seated once again at his private table in an alcove of the Gold Tip Hotel dining room, Lobo Hines looked like a man who'd been gut-punched. With trembling hands, he reached out and shoved away the plate of half-eaten breakfast on the white linen before him. "Somebody get me a drink. Whiskey!" he demanded in a raspy voice.

From where she sat to Lobo's right, Sarina Lopez made an impatient gesture to a waiter hovering attentively close by. "You heard him. Bring a bottle from the bar—and be quick about it."

Balling his fists atop the table to help control the trembling, Lobo planted a baleful gaze on the fidgeting man who stood before his table. This dusty, battered-looking, somewhat breathless individual was named Art Hicks. He was a veteran Gun Wolf, one of the first to arrive as part of Lobo's crew when he came to take over the town. This morning it had fallen to him to interrupt the boss's breakfast with some very bad news.

"Tell me again how it happened," Lobo said, his

voice still raspy, barely above a whisper. "Tell me again how you can be certain Burt Kelson is dead."

Hicks had removed his hat and was holding it in front of him like a shield, twisting it nervously in his hands. "They hit us only about a mile or so out of town," he began. "There's a spot where the hills rise up to a kind of rocky ridge with a natural gap cut through it. That's where they were waitin'. Their trail was clear up to that point so Burt and Tibbets were leadin' ahead steady, wantin' to eat up distance and close on 'em as fast as we could. They waited until we were full into the gap, then opened up on the front end. That's when I saw Burt go down right away. The whole side of his head was...well, it was clear he wasn't ever gettin' back up."

Hicks paused for a moment, seeing Lobo visibly cringe at the words, before he continued. "Tibbets went down right away, too. Then everything turned to pure hell. Bullets were flying everywhere, horses were screamin' and buckin'. Men were fallin'... There was no cover to take, so when we tried to turn and ride back out the way we came in, there were shooters waitin' on the back side of the cut, too...The only way me and the others who made it out managed, was that we were in the middle of the pack and when the powder smoke and dust got so thick, we were able to bust clear."

"How many?" Lobo wanted to know. "You said three of you made it out?"

"That's right," Hicks replied dully. "Me, Jasper Stone, and Bob Streeter. Both of them are shot up some, Streeter pretty bad...I had some boys take 'em both over to Doc Gaines, but I ain't so sure Streeter's gonna make it."

The waiter returned with a bottle of whiskey and a

glass. Lobo shoved away the glass, took the bottle and lifted it for a long pull. Lowering it, he glared straight ahead, seemingly at nothing in particular. "Burt Kelson," he said, again in raspy half-whisper. "He rode at my side for...God, almost as far back as I can remember. Before Pickaxe, before the Gun Wolves...This is a sad, sorry day, but with no wound deeper than the loss of Burt. Him and seven others."

"Nine," corrected Sarina. "You'd already lost a man last night. And another wounded."

"That's right. Nine total dead, three wounded...and one of them maybe not going to survive." Lobo took another pull from the bottle. "Jesus Christ, what a black day!"

Hicks looked equally distraught. "You want I should round up some men and head out again after the bushwhackin' skunks responsible? They can't have gone far by now."

"Tempting as that is, no." Lobo scowled fiercely. "We've still got a town to run and protect. Other interests...I'll have to send word to Denver and Cheyenne, spread notice for men to build the Gun Wolves back up again. At the same time I'll put money on the heads of those murderous bastards who bled us so low. It may take time, but I'll have their goddamn heads before I'm through. I swear it for Burt Kelson's sake, as well as the others who paid!"

"Try to calm down," Sarina said, placing a hand gently on Lobo's arm. "The first thing you need to do is bring in the bodies of Kelson and the others for a decent burial. Then you need to think about the bigger picture and to plan accordingly. As bad as this is, it's like you said—you have many other interests to consider."

Lobo started to raise the bottle to his mouth once more but stopped without taking a drink. "You're right. I've got to keep a clear head and think things through carefully." He sat the bottle back on the table and expelled a long, ragged breath. He gaze returned to Hicks. "Art, first check and see how Streeter is doing. Then go ahead and gather all the rest of the men. Not to ride out again, though. Just get them over to the barroom, including Mel Dekker. But no drinking. I'll meet with everybody once you've got them assembled..."

CHAPTER THIRTY

While Lobo was calling for a meeting in Pickaxe, another meeting was starting to take shape out at the Walburn farm. A handful of men were already present when Lone and the others returned from their ambush. Due to the limited space inside the Walburn house and the fact Billy Doyle was still recuperating in there, the middle bay of the barn was serving to accommodate the gathering.

Among those already on hand were gray-whiskered Noah Felton and John Doyle, Billy's father. It was they who had ridden through much of the night to sound the alarm calling for this get-together, though the energy of the moment left neither appearing notably the worse for wear.

Felton, perhaps because of his age and possibly also due to his farm apparently being somewhat larger and more successful than the others, seemed to be looked upon as a sort of leader for this outlying community. As an indication of his wisdom, he was quick to acknowledge what Lone and Velda had to offer when it came to dealing with the kind of matter under discussion—especially upon hearing how successful the ambush had turned out.

"I'm an old man no longer easily impressed," he stated after they'd given their report. "But there's no other word for what you so boldly set out to do and accomplished. What's more, it serves as yet another indicator that the time is right for the rest of us gathering here to rise up and finally take a stand against that which we've allowed to grind us down for too long. With their force cut nearly in half, we're never going to find Lobo and his Gun Wolves more vulnerable... My only question is this: Will you, McGantry and Miss Velda, stick with us to help see it the rest of the way through?"

Lone and Velda exchanged looks. That was sufficient, no need for words.

Turning to Felton, Lone said, "The short answer is yes. You'll remember Velda and me sayin' that our reasons for coming here in the first place already had us on a course likely to butt heads with Lobo and his Wolves. Some of those reasons still need taken care of, so continuin' to side with you only makes sense. I'll let Reese and Dutton speak for themselves, but they were an important part of our success a little while ago and I'm thinkin' you can probably count on more from them, too."

"That's a fact. Figure us in," Reese confirmed.

"The other thing you need to figure on," Lone picked up again, "is that our part in this is a little different from those of you who have homes and families at stake. You're all in it for the long haul; us four are more or less passin' through. So, I'd advise you to make sure you're prepared to do whatever it takes—meanin' to be as bold and bloody as we were against those we just dealt with—in order to see this through to the end. If you want to continue livin' here afterwards—especially if you align with us, after what we did—you're gonna have to be willin' to crush Lobo and his bunch all the way. You leave even a piece of him, he's the kind who'll pull himself back together out of hate and pure meanness and return for revenge. Hard revenge... You understand what I'm sayin'?"

Felton looked around at Doyle, Walburn, and the others grouped with him. Bringing his eyes back to Lone, he said, "I think you've stated your case pretty clearly. I'll admit my initial thought, my great, driving concern, stemmed mainly from keeping the rifles Lobo had brought in out of the hands of renegade Indians. But you're right, of course, we have to think bigger than that. We'd never get them away from Lobo anyway without some kind of confrontation, so that's a fact we have to face. And since Lobo is hardly the type to engage in a limited confrontation over a single matter...well, as I said, you paint the resulting picture clearly."

"What about the idea of seizing the rifles and destroying 'em?" said a beefy, blond-haired man Lone remembered being addressed as Mendenhall the prior day at the Milestone funeral. "Wouldn't that solve the worry about them falling into the hands of the Injuns without us getting in an all-out war with Lobo and his Wolves?"

"Jesus, Mendenhall," groaned Walburn. "Do you think Lobo would just shrug off having his guns taken and blown up? You don't think that might just make him a little bit mad and cause him to send his Wolves for retaliation?"

"I thought we were going to disguise ourselves, keep from getting recognized," Mendenhall argued.

One of the other men, a scrawny number with limp, greasy hair and piercing blue eyes who Lone didn't remember seeing before, sneered, "How much difference you think that would make to Lobo? He'd lash out in a swath sure to kill and punish enough of us to make sure he got some of who was responsible. Hell, come to think of it, it wouldn't be above him to start torturing until he got some specific names...No, Felton and McGantry are right. If we're finally gonna make this fight, we gotta be ready to take it all the way to the finish."

"Hold on. Back up a minute," interjected Velda. "What did you say before, Walburn—about blowing up the rifles?"

Walburn blinked under the directness of her question. "It was just a notion. One of the ideas we were kicking around. Like Mendenhall said, a way to destroy the guns to make sure Loo wouldn't be able to make his trade with the Indians."

"How were you going to blow them up?"

Walburn pointed to a waist high, slant-topped wooden storage bin built over against one wall. The cover was propped open with a two-by-four and the open maw of the seemingly empty insides was streaked with cobwebs. "In there," he said. "I got a box with six or eight sticks of dynamite left in it. They're left over from when I was clearing fields mostly by myself and used 'em to blow clusters of rock or stubborn tree stumps."

"How old are they? Are they still any good?"

"Don't see why they wouldn't be." Walburn twisted his mouth wryly. "I wouldn't want to light one and then hold on, betting it was too old and dried up to blow."

Lone and Velda exchanged looks again.

Lone said, "I gotta tell you, havin' some dynamite at our disposal conjures up some real interestin' possibilities."

"If blowing up the rifles is still one of them," Velda replied, "you realize of course they're stolen property most likely belonging to the U.S. Army."

Lone shrugged. "No problem. Let 'em send the bill to Lobo...if they can find enough pieces of him."

CHAPTER THIRTY-ONE

By the time the rest of the farmers and ranchers willing to participate in taking a stand against the Gun Wolves had arrived at Walburn's barn, it was nearly noon and the storm that had been moving in from the northwest had also arrived. It wasn't raining yet but the sky was a mass of churning, steadily darkening clouds with ominous growls of thunder and lightning flashes drawing closer and more frequent.

Counting Lone, Velda, Reese, and Dutton, those gathered totaled eleven. This included young Lee Walburn, who was adamant about being part of the force. A plan for how they were going to proceed had been formulated and agreed to by all present. Lone and Velda had led on the formulation, with worthwhile input from Felton, Doyle, and the scrawny, greasy-haired man who went by the name Simon and claimed experience as a sniper in the recent war and, more recently, as a buffalo hunter for the railroads. The powerful, well-maintained .50 caliber "Big Fifty" Sharps rifle he came armed with gave reasonably convincing credence to his claim.

All of the other men also came with rifles, mostly common hunting models, a couple shotguns. Two of them also had war experience. None had sidearms or professed any degree of skill with such. From the weapons they'd stripped off the ambushed Gun Wolves, Reese and Dutton distributed upgrades to those who needed improved weaponry.

The plan for the assault on the town required a measure of close timing but otherwise was basically straightforward and simple. The unexpected turn of bad weather was seen as a bit of an advantage as it made it likely the Gun Wolves would be found hunkered indoors, probably one of the two saloons or the brothel they were known to frequent, rather than roaming more widely about.

The time to get started had been reached. The final piece of business to be conducted in the barn was finishing the meal of sandwiches and hot coffee prepared and served by Letty Walburn and two other wives who'd accompanied their husbands this far.

"Well," announced Noah Felton, lowering his cup after taking the final swallow of its contents, "I guess I'm the first piece who needs to make a move on this chess board we've blocked out. Me and Ralston. Once we're out of the way, the rest of you will have your own maneuvering to begin."

"Godspeed to you, Noah," said John Doyle. "Take care, and we'll see you at three o'clock on the creek bend."

Felton's response was delayed by a particularly loud and drawn-out peal of thunder. When it was quiet enough for him to be heard again, he said with a wistful half smile, "Let's hope none of us drown between now and then. Be sure to stay on this side of the creek when you get there."

The opening move of the plan they'd put together called for Felton, accompanied by his hired man Ralston, to go into town for a visit to Dr. Gaines. The alleged reason for the visit was to seek treatment for an attack of gout, which Felton was known to suffer on a recurring basis. The real truth behind the call was for Gaines to pass on where the rifles from Hightower's wagon had been taken and also report on how many townsmen could be counted on to support the move against Lobo, details the doctor had been tasked with determining once he'd gotten back to town.

Armed with this information, Felton and Ralston would then slip unnoticed (an exit now expected to be made easier by the timely storm) out the back side of town to meet with Doyle and Walburn and the rest at a narrow, nameless creek that twisted through an otherwise empty slice of countryside. From there, they would proceed to carry out one of the main parts of their assault—setting a dynamite charge and blowing up the rifles. Whatever else transpired, this was seen as the one certainty they wanted to achieve, to eliminate any risk of the guns ever falling into renegade hands.

While this was taking place in whatever part of town dictated by the location of the rifles, Lone, Velda, Reese, and Dutton would be taking up positions at the northeast end of the community, behind the Gold Tip Hotel. When the time was right, they too would be setting off a dynamite charge—on the rear of the hotel barroom. Amidst the chaos and diversion thus created, they would then surge into a different part of the structure, a series of basement chambers where Dr. Gaines described he had been taken to tend the traumatized Hope Hightower. They meant to rescue the girl and, with a little luck, also find the Milestone sisters in the same area and free them too. And if, as part of blasting their way clear of the escalating melee, they happened to catch sight of Turk Mitchum long enough to put a bullet in him, that would be a cherry on the cake.

"In order of importance," Velda told Lone, listing the latest revision to her personal goals, "I want to free the girls, help Walburn and the others crush Lobo and his Gun Wolves, and kill Mitchum. If I never actually get to collect the bounty on him, I can live with that...On the other hand, if we help take over the town, I figure there ought to be plenty of other fugitive rats in the Gold Tip for me to collect enough bounties to retire on."

"Could be," Lone allowed. "But then what would you do for fun?"

"Easy. I'd just follow you around—things seem never to be dull wherever you are."

"I DON'T GIVE a goddamn if it is raining! You've got hats and foul weather gear, don't you?" Lobo slammed a fist onto the bar top, rattling bottles and glasses strewn down the length of it. "All the more reason to get those men off the muddy, bloody ground where they fell. Now, you've all been treated to a round of free liquor while I laid out the cold, hard facts of how Burt Kelson and seven other men were cut down in a vicious ambush. I want four volunteers to take a wagon and go bring them in—or do I have to select who, and make it an order?"

Art Hicks stepped forward from the nine men, the only remaining Gun Wolf enforcers, who were gathered in the Gold Tip barroom. "I'll go, sir," he said in a solemn tone. "I had to leave 'em behind before, nobody wants 'em brought in out of the weather and away from scavengers more than me."

Lobo gave a curt nod. "That's what I wanted to hear. You just earned yourself the spot as my new lieutenant, Hicks. The rest of you hear that clear? That's how it's gonna be from now on. Hicks will be replacing Burt. Those are some mighty big boots to fill, but I think he can measure up and I expect each and every one of you to cooperate with him fully. Especially now with our ranks cut low, we can't afford anything less."

Lobo paused and raked the room with a hard glare, looking for any sign of dissent. When he saw none, he went on. "Before the day is out I'll be sending telegrams to Cheyenne and Denver, seeking some recruits to re-strengthen our force. We all lost friends and men we've worked side by side with for quite a spell now, so I know the change may not be easy to get used to. But I'll expect full cooperation with that, too.

"In the meantime, I don't figure we'll have too much trouble keeping things running smooth until we get built back up again. Still, there might be some fool looking to test us in our depleted condition. So stay extra sharp and don't give an inch to any hint of trouble. Understood?"

Again Lobo paused and raked the room with a questioning glare. The only response he got was from outside, a crackle of lightning followed by booming thunder. Wind-whipped rain slapped against the barroom windows that were patched over with wooden boards in several places to replace the glass broken out during the previous evening's gunfight.

Lobo let his glare linger for a minute on the broken windows before addressing Hicks once more. "Alright, go ahead then. Pick the men you want to take with you, disperse the others how you want. Be sure to put at least one back on Hightower at Doc Gaines' place. And tell him to let the sawbones know I'll be paying him a visit myself in short order."

Hicks promptly set about following these instructions, seeming to adapt well to his command over the other men. The barroom quickly cleared out, leaving Lobo alone except for Mel Dekker.

Once the others were gone, Dekker didn't waste any time saying from under a cocked brow, "I don't make a habit of jumping like a buzzard on another hombre's misfortune, but I gotta say, old chum, I kinda thought I might rate a shot at taking over Kelson's position."

Lobo eyed him in return. "Yeah. I guess it shouldn't surprise me you might feel that way."

"Well?"

Lobo took a bottle from the bar, poured some in a glass, drank it unhurriedly. "For starters, you ain't even a regular member of our outfit, Mel. And I saw no sure signs you wanted to be. I been in operation here three, four years now and you just recently came around. That makes you kind of a late-comer, don't you think?"

"You forgetting all those past years we rode together? Then we drifted apart, you did your thing and I did mine for a while. But when I had a really big opportunity, a plan for snatching those army rifles, I came to you, didn't I?"

"Yeah, you did," Lobo admitted.

"So I *do* want to stay on as part of your outfit here," Dekker stated. "You been saying all along that the deal you're gonna make for those guns is the biggest single money-maker you ever pulled. Yeah, I might be a latecomer. But I say supplying you with the guns to make that deal possible deserves me a spot pretty damn far up in the ranks."

Lobo leaned his elbows on the bar top. "You might have a valid point...except for a couple bothersome details."

"Like what?" Dekker wanted to know.

Starting out slow and calm, but unable to hold back some bursts of loud, harsh anger, Lobo replied, "Number one, the rifles are here *but in a useless goddamned condition*! Number two, the person who can correct that problem is laid out cold as a stone because *you were stupid enough to pound his brain into pudding*!"

"Now wait a minute. You can't blame me for that," Dekker protested. "If that sneaky lowdown preacher hadn't messed with those guns in the first place then—"

"Shut up!" Lobo cut him off. "Blaming him for what he did don't change what you did to make it worse." He turned his head slowly and looked Dekker square in the face, the Gun Wolf boss's eyes glowing as feral as those of the wild animal he was called after. "And if Hightower don't wake up, if he dies and this whole deal falls apart... I'm going to blame you *real hard*, old chum."

CHAPTER THIRTY-TWO

"FOUR MORE...WE CAN'T HARDLY PASS THAT UP, CAN WE?" Velda kept her voice low, just loud enough to be heard above the hiss of rain and in between growls of thunder.

"No, I reckon not," Lone replied. But there was a reluctance evident in his voice, even before he added, "I gotta say, though, it sticks in my craw some."

"What do you mean?"

Reese knew the answer. "Pretty old tradition to let the enemy carry off his dead and wounded, even in the most brutal war."

Nobody said anything for a minute. The only sounds were those of the ongoing storm.

Upon reaching the ambush site on their way back to town, Lone, Velda, Reese, and Dutton had encountered unexpected activity up ahead in the middle of the cut through the rocky ridge. Only the noise and mid-day gloom of the storm had prevented their approach from being spotted in return. Once they'd held back and were able to discern through the pouring rain what was taking place, they recognized it as a retrieval by four men (certainly other Gun Wolves) of the dead bodies left in the wake of the ambush.

Finally, heaving a sigh, Lone spoke again. "The thing is, though, every one of those snakes we stomp out before the farmers or ranchers ever have to face 'em, means improved odds for keepin' down the loss of decent lives. And tradition or not, the whole pack of Gun Wolves ain't worth even a bullet burn on any of the good men finally willin' to stand up against 'em."

"So how do we play it?" Velda wanted to know.

Wiping rain from his face, Lone said, "We confront 'em. Allow 'em a chance to surrender. I expect they'll be too ornery to take it...But we will have tried."

"I can go with that," responded Reese.

Velda and Dutton signaled agreement with their silence.

THEY WAITED until all but one of the bodies had been loaded onto the flatbed wagon drawn by a team of mules. Two men were up on the wagon, arranging the bodies neatly and respectfully after they were handed up by two other men on the ground.

Hoisting loose-limbed, dead weight bodies, made soggy and slippery and even heavier by the drenching rain, was no easy task. The four bedraggled individuals involved in the final stage of this were obviously exhausted and worn down.

That's when Lone and the others rushed in on horseback, arms extended to clearly display their drawn guns.

"Freeze right like you are!" Lone shouted. "Go ahead

and lay down that last body, then stand tall and still with your hands raised in plain sight."

The Gun Wolves froze in awkward, uncertain poses as the riders swarmed in closer and formed a semicircle around the end of the wagon. "What is this? Do you know who you're messin' with?" demanded Art Hicks, one of the men up on the flatbed.

"We know exactly," Velda snapped in reply.

Hicks' rain-spattered face showed delayed recognition and then twisted with sudden rage. "You! You're the bitch—you and the rest—who bushwhacked us this morning!"

"That's right. And if you survived that, then you ought to be smart enough not to press your luck a second time," Velda told him.

But, just like Lone predicted, the new lieutenant of the Gun Wolves wasn't having any. His rage and sense of desperation—and maybe something deeper inside that urged him to try and live up to his newly acquired status—wouldn't let him.

Shouting, "It's no good, boys—they're out to kill us sure!" Hicks clawed frantically for the hogleg holstered on his hip as he simultaneously spun to one side and tried to leap for cover off the edge of the wagon.

This reaction from him left the other Wolves little choice but to make their own futile attempts at resistance.

And that left Lone and the others no choice but to do what they had to.

Once again the scene rang with gunfire. The reports of pistols barked back against the booming rolls of thunder from overhead and new bodies quickly joined those of the men who'd fallen earlier. Hicks was riddled with bullets while still in midair from his leap off the wagon, his life gone before he ever hit the ground. The other three fared no better. Not one of them even managed to clear leather before they were hammered down by a hail of lead.

CHAPTER THIRTY-THREE

"WAS THAT LOBO I SAW LEAVING HERE WHEN WE WERE riding up?" asked Noah Felton as he limped into Dr. Gaines office, followed by Ralston.

"Yeah, it was," replied the doc. "Come on in, get out of your wet wraps and then let's step into my secondary treatment room." He waited for the two men to begin peeling off their foul weather gear and then added, "Even though that man standing out on the front porch is stationed to watch full time, Lobo feels the need to come around himself and check regularly on how Reverend Hightower is doing."

"How is he doing?" asked Felton.

Gaines hesitated long enough to glance at the front door, on the other side of which stood the aforementioned man posted by Lobo. Even though the drumming rain had a muffling effect on any conversation inside, the doctor still kept his voice low. "No change so far...at least none Lobo is aware of."

Once he and Ralston had hung their soaked wraps on pegs in the outer office and followed Gaines into his spare treatment room (the main one being occupied by Hightower), Felton said also in a lowered voice, "What did you mean by no change 'Lobo is aware of'?"

Gaines smiled slyly. "Just what I said...The truth is, the reverend showed signs of coming around not too long ago. I made the decision to keep him under a while longer with some chloroform."

"Why do that?"

"First, sit down and put your leg up so it looks like I'm examining it in case anybody walks in unexpected."

Felton scowled. "Is that really necessary?"

"With so much at stake, let's not take any chances," Gaines told him.

Felton went ahead and lowered himself onto the examining chair and placed one foot up on a stool. Then he said, "Better yet, what if Ralston waited out in the front office to give us warning in case anybody shows up?"

"Okay by me if it's okay with Ralston."

"Got it covered," said the hired man. "I'll be close, holler if you need me for anything."

Once Ralston had stepped back into the other room, Gaines explained, "Having so much at stake is the same reason I thought it best to continue keeping Hightower out of it at this stage of things. All we need is for him to wake up and, before he has full awareness, blurt out something that might cause Lobo to go off halfcocked in some way disruptive to how everything is set in motion...It *is* underway, correct?"

"Indeed it is," Felton stated firmly.

Gaines looked relieved. "When I heard how effective the ambush by McGantry and Velda was, I didn't see any way but for the momentum to only build. As a doctor, a healer, I suppose I ought to be remorseful for such a high loss of life. But when I consider how it was a toll taken on men who've all participated in bullying, beating, raping, and killing over the past years...more of the same probably, in places we don't even know about...it's hard not to think that the world is better off without them."

"It is, Doc. That's the only way to look at it," Felton assured him. "And, like I told the men back at Walburn's, never before could we have hoped to find Lobo and his Gun Wolves this vulnerable."

"The report I heard was eight killed in the ambush. Then one of the two wounded who were brought in, died on me. And another killed last night." Gaines looked grim. "That's ten dead, two still badly wounded. Near as I can figure, there can't be more than nine or ten fully functioning Gun Wolves left to deal with."

Felton nodded. "That's about what we figure, too. We also expect there might be a handful of fugitives Lobo is harboring in the Gold Tip who'll join in to help him. So there'll still be plenty of scoundrels to go around. But here's the plan we finalized to deal with them..."

A quarter hour later, Felton had laid out the assault plan for Gaines. The doctor, in turn, had provided Felton with all the information he'd been tasked to gather for those mounting the assault. The key part of this was the location of where the rifles had been moved to—this being, logically enough, a warehouse owned by Lobo and located behind the Lucky Nugget saloon, also owned by Hines and a favored watering hole of the Gun Wolves.

A final piece of welcome information served up by

Gaines was that he'd gotten verbal buy-in from half a dozen businessmen around town who were willing to support the farmers and ranchers if it came to a shootout against Lobo and his men. They'd be waiting and watching from their store windows, armed and ready to take part at the first sign of lead starting to fly.

In order to identify friend from foe when things broke loose, especially given the blurred visibility presented by the storm, Gaines came up with the suggestion that all working *against* the Gun Wolves mark themselves by tying a bright red bandanna around their left upper arm. The businessmen all liked the idea and agreed to adopt it. So did Felton, for which the doctor supplied him a fistful of red bandannas to hand out to the others when he and Ralston re-joined them.

"Toward that end," Felton announced when everything had been gone over, "we'd best be on our way to make the rendezvous. We're supposed to meet the others at the creek by three. The target time for setting off the explosions is three-thirty."

"That should work out well," Gaines said. "The warehouse is on the same side of town as the creek and, given the uselessness of the rifles in their present condition and the fact the Gun Wolves are now so undermanned, I'd bet it's not very heavily guarded."

Felton lowered his leg and stood up. "Let's hope so. Our men will approach it with caution all the same. I trust the townsmen will recognize the explosions as the signal things are underway?"

"I told them that, although it wasn't a certainty, using dynamite was being strongly discussed the last I knew. When things start blowing up, I think they'll get the message loud and clear."

Felton took a step toward the door but then paused to eye the medic with a very direct look. "What about you, Doc? Are you going to join in?"

Gaines met his gaze with a grave expression settling over his face. "I've been asking myself that same question all day," he said. "I'm torn between my oath to heal and not do harm, and the tremendous hypocrisy I would be showing if I merely stood back and let others do what I have encouraged...In the end I've decided that, after you leave here, I will go out into the front office and remove the old Dragoon pistol I keep in a drawer of my desk. If, when the trouble starts, that vulture Lobo has posted on my front porch remains in place long enough, I'll do my best to eliminate him in the interest of preventing the harm he might do to someone else."

Felton's mouth pulled into a tight, straight line. "I know what a hard decision that must be for you, Doc. I admire you for making it...Just be sure you don't get harmed in the process."

CHAPTER THIRTY-FOUR

LOBO HINES HAD JUST EXITED THE TELEGRAPH OFFICE when he noticed the wagon coming down the street. It seemed to be headed toward Wilkes' livery, which wasn't unusual. It was somewhat surprising, however, that anybody would be industrious enough to be out and about with a heavy, flatbed work wagon in such harsh weather. The wind and thunder had abated some, but a cold, steady rain was continuing to pour straight down and flashes of lightning still flickered across the sooty gray sky.

Lobo flipped his collar up against the rain and paused to see if he recognized whoever was on the driver's seat, foolishly braving these miserable conditions. It was only then that he belatedly realized there was *no one* at the reins of the rig, it was just rolling along pulled by a plodding team of mules headed instinctively back to the shelter of the livery barn. Lobo's next delayed realization came when he made a more careful scan, through the murky rain, at the cargo loaded on the wagon—and a jolt ran through him like a pitchfork of lightning had struck from above.

"Good God Almighty!" he exclaimed, hurling himself from the boardwalk in front of the telegraph office and half-running, half-staggering out into the muddy street. "Wilkes! Wilkes!" he shouted, trying to catch up with the team as they continued plodding toward the livery only a short ways farther on the opposite side. "Get hold of these goddamned hammerheads! Stop them!"

One of the livery barn's doors swung open and a bewildered looking Ebediah Wilkes stood there in baggy bib overalls, holding a three-tine hay fork. "What in blazes is goin' on?" he called out. A moment later he saw the mules headed toward him and, beyond, the running, wailing figure of the Gun Wolf boss.

"Grab that team! Pull them inside!" Lobo shouted.

Obediently, Wilkes tossed aside the hay fork and moved forward to intercept the mules, reaching to seize the bridle of the nearest one and steady it to a halt. It took a minute longer to reach back and push the barn doors open wider so the team and wagon could go on in, the animals doing so eagerly in order to get out of the rain.

A drenched, panting Lobo soon followed. He lurched to one side of the wagon and sagged against it, his face a mask of agony as his eyes swept over the grisly cargo of dead bodies heaped on the flatbed before him. Lanterns hung on posts to either side of the barn bay, lighted to offset the gloom of the storm, cast an eerie, shadowy illumination over the sight. "Oh my God," Lobo groaned. "Look at my poor, brave men...All shot to hell and slaughtered! Where's the mercy?"

Moving up from the front of the mule team, Wilkes got his first look at what the wagon was carrying. It staggered him. "Jesus! What is this? I can't have that in here!"

"Shut up," Lobo snapped, turning a fierce scowl on him. "Are you saying your stinking horse barn is too good for these brave souls?"

"N-no. I didn't mean that," stammered Wilkes. "It's just that...What happened? What's going on?"

"Assassins! Merciless assassins!" Lobo declared. And then his gaze fell on the contorted, upturned face of Art Hicks. His eyes tracked down the bullet-riddled torso, seeing where blood had tried to pool in the gaping wounds but was now washed by the rain to just watery, pinkish smears. "No!" he gasped, taking a step back. "Not you too, Hicks...More slaughter!"

Lobo's reaction caused Wilkes to look even more bewildered and alarmed. "What's happening?" he said again.

His own expression turning suddenly from one of anguish to the look of a predator sensing his own danger, Lobo hissed, "They're out to destroy me!" His right hand flashed inside his vest and reappeared gripping the Colt Lightning. "Quick! Dowse those lanterns, pull those doors back shut!"

As he moved to assist with the latter, Lobo had barely reached the gaping doorway when a jarring roar —much louder and sharper than any of the waning thunder—sounded from somewhere up the street. Accompanying this, even as Lobo' eyes darted to try and pinpoint the source of the noise, a brilliant red-gold flash appeared and blossomed behind the silhouettes of some buildings the Gun Wolf boss had no trouble identifying.

"My saloon! My warehouse!" he blurted in a strangled voice.

And then, before he had any chance to recover from that, another roar of sound ripped apart the stormy afternoon and another brilliant red-gold flash sliced through the pouring rain from up near the end of the street.

"*My hotel!*"

IN A SHALLOW DITCH twenty yards behind the Hines warehouse, where he had scrambled to after lighting the fuse on the six-stick dynamite charge that had just gone off, Fred Walburn hunkered low with his son Lee and Noah Felton, waiting for the blast debris to stop clattering down around them. As that was coming to an end, in the distance they heard the distinct roar of another explosion—the one touched off on the Gold Tip barroom.

"There goes Lone and his crew, right on time," Walburn said excitedly. Rising up and squinting through the rain at the flames and smoke billowing out of a ragged hole where the back wall of the warehouse had once been, he was pleased to be able to make out the heap of twisted gun barrels and splintered stocks on the other side. "That did it," he announced in the same excited tone. "We're in the thick of it now—there's no turning back even if we wanted to."

"I think you'd be hard pressed to find any of our

men who *did* want to," stated Felton. "The only thing left is to keep going and finish it."

"Exactly," agreed Walburn, pulling himself and his Henry rifle out of the ditch. "I'm going to go join the others for our sweep up the street. You two drop back and guard the horses in case things don't go well and we're forced to make a retreat."

"Are you sure I can't go with you, Pa?" pleaded Lee.

His father gave a firm shake of his head. "This was all agreed to. We each have our roles. Now go with Noah. Anybody comes nosing around back here not wearing a red bandanna, you know what to do."

FROM BEHIND ONE of the twin outhouses out back of the Gold Tip Hotel, Lone and Velda peered around to view with satisfaction the smoldering, splintered gash that had until moments earlier been the outside rear corner of the establishment's barroom. A spray of blurred lantern light stabbed out through the swirling smoke and pelting rain, mingling with the frantic wailing and cursing of those who'd been inside when the dynamite charge went off.

"I think we may have spilled a few drinks," Velda remarked.

"They may not know it, but I expect there's some in there who are lucky they didn't get their blood spilled and gone for a ride on that wagon we sent rolling through town a little bit ago," said Lone.

"If that's the case," spoke up Reese as he and Dutton stepped out from behind the other outhouse, "leave 'em for me and Dut to go in and take care of. Maybe we'll get lucky, too, and our bouncer friends will be among 'em. Either way, you two hightail it off and find those basement chambers in order to free the girls...We'll meet you somewhere in the middle."

"See that you do," Lone responded crisply. "Watch each other's back and don't hesitate to ventilate anybody who looks even a little bit wrong."

CHAPTER THIRTY-FIVE

SKIDDING AND SLIPPING ON THE WET, MUDDY GROUND AS he made his way frantically along the back alley that ran from Wilkes' livery up behind the row of various businesses that lined the west side of Pickaxe's main street, Lobo finally reached the structure that housed the Dust Cutter Saloon, one of the two beer joints he owned. Drenched and breathing hard, still brandishing the Colt Lightning, he entered in through the rear and barged out into the barroom. The scene that met his eyes did little to settle his rattled condition.

Up at the front windows—which showed gaping holes in several places—two round-topped tables had been turned up on their sides and a man with a drawn hogleg was crouched behind each. Lobo recognized the men as two of his long-standing Gun Wolf enforcers, Jasper Gilby and Dakota Tucker. They appeared poised for trading lead with somebody out in the street.

In between the front windows and where Lobo had entered, a pair of frightened-looking customers, elderly men, were hunkered under a table where they'd apparently been sitting when things broke loose. Over behind the bar, the stick man Tubby Dean was ducked down along with a painted-up doxie in a spangled dress. Tubby was gripping a sawed-off shotgun but was showing not the slightest sign of eagerness to try and put it to use.

Lobo made a stooped-over rush to the end of the bar and crouched down there. "Tubby, what's going on? What the hell happened?" he wanted to know, and then winced when he realized he sounded like Ebediah Wilkes.

"I don't know, Mr. Hines," Tubby answered. "First there was some kind of explosion across the street and then, a minute later, gunfire started popping all over the place."

Lobo leaned out and called toward the front. "Gilby, this Lobo—What can you see out there? What the hell's going on?"

"I don't know what to make of it, Boss. It's like some kind of attack," came the answer.

"Attack by who?"

"I can't tell. All I know is there was an explosion catty-corner across the street, behind the Lucky Nugget. When I poked my head out to see what that was all about, there was another explosion up at the Gold Tip. Then, next thing I know, bullets are busting out the window right next to me."

"There's somebody over in the boot shop doorway who can't shoot for sour apples," said Tucker from behind the other table. "But there's another sumbitch in the side alley just a ways down who's poppin' with what sounds like a Big Fifty—and he's raisin' holy hell."

Right on the heels of that, several gunshots crackled

out in the street and a bullet smacked the window sill a couple feet above Tucker's head. The Wolf dropped low for a moment, then bobbed up and triggered two quick rounds of his own. "There!" he crowed, dropping back down again, "I think I got at least a piece of that boot shop skunk!"

A moment after that a resounding boom sounded from outside and a heavy slug blew away another huge chunk of window glass before sailing across the room and destroying a half dozen bottles of liquor on a shelf behind the bar. The painted doxie screamed and pressed herself even tighter to the floor. Tubby's bulk prevented him from scrunching any lower than he already was.

"There's that sumbitch with the Big Fifty again—I'd sure like to get a bead on him!" cursed Tucker.

"What's this all about, Boss?" Gilby wanted to know.

"I wish I knew," Lobo responded through gritted teeth. "I'm beginning to think some gang must be trying to take over our operation. At first I thought it was all that horse thief and his girlfriend—but there's more to it than just them."

"There sure is! There are shooters on this side of the street, too. If I didn't know better, I'd think some of 'em might even be the store owners. Whoever it is, they're pouring lead into the Lucky Nugget. I think that's Oscar Honeywell over there, firing back. I don't know if there's anybody else in there with him or not."

"What about up at the hotel?" asked Lobo. "Can you see what's going on there?"

"Not from here, no. Like I said, I know there was an explosion and now I can hear gunfire up that way, too. That's all I can tell."

"Damn!" Lobo spat.

More slugs peppered the front of the saloon.

"Tucker," Lobo called. "Can you hold down things here if I take Gilby with me? I've got to make it up to the Gold Tip—Sarina is bound to be in danger."

"Go ahead," Tucker called back. "I want to stick around long enough to finish having it out with Mr. Big Fifty anyway."

Lobo nodded, even though Tucker wasn't looking his way. "Good. Gilby, work your way back here, we'll go out the rear." Then, leaning to look around behind the bar, he said, "Tubby, give me that sawed-off and a handful of shells. You sure as hell aren't going to put them to any use."

A minute later, he and Gilby were on their way out the back. Gilby paused to call over his shoulder, "Keep your head down, Tuck—and give 'em hell!"

IN A SIDE ALLEY just up from the Lucky Nugget, Fred Walburn announced himself and then slipped in beside where Vern Mendenhall was crouched behind a big wooden rain barrel at the mouth of the alley. The continuing rain had the barrel filled to overflowing but an already thoroughly drenched Mendenhall seemed not to notice.

"I hear a lot of shooing, how's it going out there?" Walburn asked.

"We got things poppin', that's for sure," Mendenhall replied. "Doyle and Riley O'Keefe made for the other side of the street. I covered 'em. Doyle made it okay and is over there shootin' out of the print shop. O'Keefe took a bullet, though. He went down but managed to scramble in behind that water trough across the way. I couldn't tell how bad he got hit, but he hasn't shown himself since."

"Damn!" Walburn said. Then, peering through the rain, he added, "Okay, I see the shots comin' out of the print shop. But it looks like two shooters. Who else is in there with Doyle?"

"It's Dobbs, that pipsqueak little printer himself. He's blastin' away right along with Doyle. Can you beat it? They got somebody pinned down in the Lucky Nugget."

"Maybe I should circle back and try to get in behind whoever that is."

"Be mighty careful if you do," advised Mendenhall. "That Simon fella with the big buffalo gun was aimin' to work his way in from the other side. But right now he's helpin' me and somebody up by the boot shop make things hot for those boys over in the Dust Cutter."

Walburn grimaced. "Even more reason I should try my luck while you all are busy with that."

"Your call. Watch your tail feathers if you try it."

A SHORT WAYS farther up the street, Dr. Gaines stood just inside the open front door to his office. In his hand he held a long-barreled Colt Dragoon revolver, a curl of smoke still wafting up from its muzzle. With his face locked in a somber expression, the doctor's flat gaze was angled down at the still form of a man sprawled on the edge of the boardwalk immediately outside his doorway. The man, the watchdog posted by Lobo, had fallen in such a way that his feet and legs remained on the boardwalk while his torso, splayed arms, and head were out in the street. His hat, knocked off when he fell, lay upside down beside his head and was rapidly filling with rainwater; in death, his wide open eyes were staring straight up, unblinking in the same downpour.

As he continued to stare down at the man he'd killed, Gaines replayed the act in his mind. How, at the report of the second explosion, he'd opened the door and stood in the opening. The watchdog, his body poised in alarm and his gun hand already clamped on the six-shooter holstered at his hip, was whipping his head first one way and then the other, looking up and down the street.

At the sound of the door opening behind him, he'd spun around wearing a half-bewildered, half-suspicious scowl and said, "What the hell's going on?"

"Only this," Gaines had replied calmly. Then he'd raised the Dragoon and pulled the trigger.

With it all still so raw and fresh in his mind and the victim sprawled so clearly right there before him, the doctor felt a curious lack of emotion. If anything, he felt relief. Relief that he had acted, had gone ahead and followed through on the decision that had come with such difficulty.

As he continued standing there in the doorway, listening to the escalating bark of gunfire cutting through the drumming rain, the sense of relief grew stronger in him. What he was hearing was the sound of the decent people of Pickaxe and its surrounding area at last starting to heal themselves. Heal themselves from a disease that had infected them for too long...The disease of Lobo Hines and his Gun Wolves.

CHAPTER THIRTY-SIX

LONE AND VELDA BARGED INTO THE KITCHEN AREA OF THE Gold Tip's dining room with drawn guns. The handful of cooks and servers milling there, already alarmed and half-panicked by the explosion and now the sound of gunfire breaking out over in the barroom, were certainly not calmed by the sight of them.

Sensing their fear and wanting to take full advantage of it, Lone waved his Colt with a flourish and called out, "Nobody do anything stupid and you won't get hurt! We're here to harm some folks right enough, but it don't have to be any of you unless you give us cause."

Half a dozen sets of bugged eyes followed the Colt's muzzle as it swept over them, but otherwise the owners of those eyes held totally still.

"We need somebody to show us the quickest way down into the basement," Lone went on. "Then the rest of you should scatter and scatter wide—'Cause like I said, there *is* gonna be trouble here."

More gunfire sounded from the direction of the barroom.

"You," Velda said, pointing her sixer at a pencil-mustached individual wearing a stained cook's apron. "You know the way to the basement?"

The man's over-sized Adam's apple bobbed up and down under his bony chin before he stammered, "Y – Yes. Yes, I can show you."

"Then lead the way and be quick about it," Lone ordered. Waving his gun again, he told the others, "The rest of you *git*! And don't look back."

The staff members thus directed were so eager to comply they nearly trampled one another crowding out the back door through which Lone and Velda had entered only a minute earlier. As the last of them scrambled out of sight, the cook in the stained apron said, "We'll have to go out into the lobby. The door that leads to the basement stairwell is behind the front desk."

"Like you said—show us." Velda made a thrusting gesture with her gun. "I shouldn't have to tell you how foolish it would be for you to try some kind of trick."

"Don't worry about that. I only work here. You can do whatever you want, just don't put a bullet in me," the cook said in a strained voice. "And to show I'm on the level, I'll warn you to be careful of the front desk clerk if he's out there... He ain't likely to be so cooperative."

"Be his hard luck if he ain't," Lone grated.

The cook led the way out the serving door and into the dining room, where no one was in sight. Since it was the middle of the afternoon, a common lag time between lunch and dinner, it was hard to say whether there'd been no diners present when things busted loose or if they had already hastily departed. In any event, Lone and Velda stayed alert continuing on the heels of the cook as he angled toward the open glass doors that fed to the lobby area separating the dining room from the barroom.

Entering the lobby, they found that it too was empty of people. All except for a balding, bullet-headed man in a string tie and patterned silk vest stationed behind the front desk. Actually, he was partially hunkered down behind it, a Remington revolver visibly clenched in one meaty fist while he warily eyed the doors to the barroom where sporadic gunfire was still taking place.

When Lone, Velda, and the cook came through the dining room doorway, the balding man's head—and also the muzzle of his Remington—swung around.

"Whoa, George!" the cook was quick to say. "It's just me."

"Claude!" George's broad face scrunched into a suspicious scowl. "What the hell are you doing out here? And who's that with you?"

Velda responded. "Sarina sent us. We're to get the girls out of the basement and take them to safety until whatever's happening is brought under control."

For a moment it looked like the distraught George might be willing to buy the falsehood. His scowl started to relax ever so slightly, but then suddenly clamped tighter still. "No, I don't believe that! Miss Sarina is still upstairs, she couldn't have—"

"You had your chance," Lone said, interrupting the clerk with words and simultaneously with a trigger pull that planted a bullet in the middle of George's bullet head. George pitched backward, the Remington dropping from his grip and clattering onto the desktop as he toppled heavily to the floor. Velda rushed forward and rounded the end of the desk to check and make sure he was dead.

"Oh, God," Claude groaned, sagging visibly at the knees.

"Is there a door back there like there's supposed to be?" Lone called to Velda.

There was a slight pause before she called back, "Yes. And it opens to a stairwell leading down."

Lone cut his gaze to the cook. "Alright, Claude. You held up you end, now beat it. Put as much distance as you can between yourself and this joint!"

IN THE SECOND floor hallway of the Gold Tip, a short distance outside her private quarters, Sarina Lopez halted in alarm. She'd already been alerted by the sound of the explosion and the reports of gunshots coming from the first floor. But they'd been somewhat muted, obviously originating at the opposite end of the building. The single gunshot and loud voices she'd heard just a moment ago, however, had been much closer, seeming to come from the lobby directly below at the mouth of the open staircase.

Sarina's glossy hair was piled to perfection and she was dressed elegantly, as always; but the chiseled features of her face were drawn tight by an expression of grave concern. Something was very wrong. The nickel-plated, over-under derringer she clutched in one delicate hand (a gift from Lobo that he insisted she always keep close) was of some comfort, but not enough. And where was Lobo, anyway?

A moment after Sarina had this thought, a doorway just up the hall from where she'd stopped suddenly burst open and Mel Dekker poked his head out, looking quickly and warily in each direction. When his gaze locked on Sarina, he said, "What's going on? Where's Lobo?"

Sarina shook her head. "I haven't the answer to either of those questions."

"Jesus, it sounds like a war's broken out downstairs!" Dekker stepped the rest of the way out into the hallway. In his left hand he held a gunbelt and empty holster, in his right the gun from the holster.

"Yes, and it sounds like it's getting closer," said Sarina.

A tousle-haired blonde Hilary filled the doorway behind Dekker and put a hand on his shoulder. "You're not going down there, are you? Why not say up here where it's safe and let somebody else handle it?"

"But what if it *doesn't* get handled, and makes its way up here?" Dekker wanted to know. "That first sound was an explosion of some kind. That could result in fire and I damn sure don't want to get trapped if a fire breaks out!"

"Now you're frightening me worse," Hilary wailed.

Before anyone could say anything further, there was the sound of boots tramping on steps. Only they weren't ascending from below, but rather were coming *down* a flight of stairs located just ahead, marking access to the hotel's third floor. Three men came hurriedly off the steps and onto the hallway landing, but then pulled up to gaze cautiously down the open staircase toward the lobby below. All three were hard-looking individuals and each was gripping a revolver with obvious familiarity.

"Hey!" one of the trio exclaimed as his face whipped

around upon sensing the presence of the hallway's other occupants.

When the narrowed, suspicious eyes of the other two swung around also, Sarina took a quick step forward to make sure they got a good look at her. While she'd only ever spent limited time in the company of any of the men, she knew they would recognize her as Lobo's woman and that would be enough to quell any sudden harsh reaction from them. She had a recollection of their names (or that which they chose to be called by) and that they were three of Lobo's 'exclusive' Gold Tip guests, meaning they were high dollar fugitives seeking the kind of haven Pickaxe's initial reputation had been built on.

Babbit, a homely, sawed-off, ill-tempered number who seemed to be carrying a grudge against the world for not turning out bigger and better looking, said, "What's with all the boomin' and bangin'? I'm payin' big money for some peace and quiet here, not to spend my afternoon over a shootin' gallery!"

"Some kind of unexpected trouble has obviously broken out. I'm sure Lobo will get it quieted down very shortly," Sarina told him.

"Where is Lobo?" asked Redfield, a stocky, moon-faced man with pleasant, soft-spoken mannerisms yet a hint of barely contained wildness in his eyes that, once detected, was quite unsettling.

"I'm not exactly sure," Sarina answered. "But I trust he is very near or perhaps already down below working on the problem."

A fresh burst of gunfire crackled, though once more somewhat muted as it again came from the other end of the building.

The third hardcase, a tall, rugged specimen who called himself Mitchum, muttered, "If that's Lobo, it sounds like he could use some help. And whether it's him or not, I don't much like the thought of getting caught up here like a bird on a perch in case the trouble comes boiling up our way."

"Now you're talking my kind of language," declared Dekker, swinging the gunbelt around his waist and buckling it in place. "Let's climb down off this perch and go see what's what!"

CHAPTER THIRTY-SEVEN

THE STAIRWELL LEADING DOWN INTO THE BASEMENT WAS narrow and dark. At the bottom was a tunnel-like hallway with boarded-over walls and heavy support beams every few yards bracing equally thick ceiling joists. There were four doors along the hall, two on each side. In the middle of these a low-burning oil lamp was attached to one of the vertical beams.

Once they reached the bottom of the steps, Lone and Velda paused briefly to survey the scene. Everything down here was still and quiet. Nothing moved and the ongoing sputter of gunfire from above was muffled even more.

After a moment, Lone walked over to the low-burning lantern and turned up its wick. In the increased wash of illumination he could see that each of the doors were equipped with heavy duty hasp locks. Three of them were fastened shut with only a simple wedged peg inserted through the locking eye. The fourth, however, was secured by a sturdy looking padlock.

Velda stepped up beside Lone and said, "If the girls

are down here, I'd say it's clear where they're being held."

Together they went to the door with the padlock. At face height there was a foot-square barred window cut into the thick slabs of the door. Lone put his face near the window and called, "Hello? Is anyone in there?"

No one answered but a faint rustling sound could be heard from the other side.

Lone called again. "We're here to help. We're lookin' for Hope Hightower...also the Milestone sisters."

After several beats, a young woman's voice said hesitantly. "We don't know you."

Sensing the owner of the frightened voice might respond better to another female, Velda crowded Lone aside and took her turn at calling in. "No, you don't know us but we're friends of your families. We know Reverend Hightower and know how he was forced to aid gunrunners because his daughter was being held captive...And we know what happened at the Milestone farm."

"And now we're here to rescue you, to get you away from here," Lone added.

A new, even more reluctant voice spoke softly from the darkness inside the room. "You know my father? Is he all right?"

"He suffered an injury. But he's going to be okay, especially after he sees you."

The first voice said, "What about our parents?"

Lone thought about it but could see no benefit in delaying the hurt by lying. He replied, "I'm sorry to have to tell you that they're dead."

Meaning to soften Lone's directness some, Velda was quick to say, "But we're working with several of your friends and neighbors who care about you very much—especially a certain fellow named Billy Doyle."

The face of a moderately pretty young woman appeared in the window. Her hands gripped the bars with white-knuckled intensity. "Billy? Is he here?"

"He's near. He played a big part in setting things in motion to rescue you."

The girl's brows pinched together. "We heard a loud boom. And then what sounds like shooting—is this what that is all about?"

"It is. But we're wastin' too much time talkn'," Lone said impatiently. "You gals in there stand back. I'm gonna open this lock."

Once he and Velda had flattened themselves against the wall, Lone placed the muzzle of his .44 to within a couple inches of the lock and triggered a round straight into it. He had to blast it a second time before the mechanism popped. Within moments he was yanking open the door and following Velda into the room, she carrying the lantern from the hall and holding it high to provide light.

The room was roughly a twelve foot square, reasonably clean, very sparsely furnished. There were three cots, each with a blanket and pillow; a chamber pot; a wash stand with a pitcher and basin; and a small table in the center with an unlighted candle propped on it. The girls were all dressed in sleeveless, loose-fitting gray shifts that reached to mid-calf; rope sandals on their feet. The Milestone sisters resembled each other, tall and slender, beginning to show some womanly curves even in their present shapeless garments, long reddish brown hair spilling over their shoulders. Hope Hightower was small and frail-looking, pale thin arms poking from her shift, but with beautiful golden hair and wide, anxious blue eyes.

"Are any of you hurt? Can you move and travel okay?" Velda wanted to know.

The uniform answer was that no, none of them were hurt and yes, they were certainly ready, willing, and able to travel if it meant getting away from here.

"Okay," said Lone. "We're goin' up the stairs with me in front, you gals next, then Velda. We'll come out in the lobby. I don't know what we'll run into there, you can hear there's still shootin' goin' on up above. But we'll do what we have to, then make our way around and out through the dining room kitchen to where we have horses waitin' out back."

"Why not use the steps that go directly outside?" questioned Hope. Then, explaining further, she said, "The next room down is a store room of some kind. I've heard men bring in supplies a number of different times since I've been here. There's got to be a stairwell of some kind over there."

And indeed there was. With Lone leading the way and Velda continuing to wield the lantern, they all hurried out and around into the adjacent room. There, after rolling aside a couple of wooden barrels and re-stacking some boxes, they found a set of stone steps cut into the back wall. These angled steeply upward and were capped at the top by a slanted cellar door that, on the outside, would have been just above ground level.

Lone entered the stairwell and climbed as far as he could. Pushing against the door, he found it was securely hinged along one side and would only lift a few inches on the other. In the gap where it lifted, he could see a segment of chain.

"Damn!" he exclaimed, dropping to one knee on a stone step. "That chain must be padlocked on the outside."

"Does that mean we're back to going out through the kitchen then?" said Velda.

"No," Lone replied through clenched teeth. "I ain't gonna give up that doggone easy!"

He re-positioned himself, planting his feet wide and a step higher than before, causing his legs to be sharply bent. Then, pressing his broad back against the bottom of the door, he pushed up, straining to straighten his legs. The door groaned and creaked and bowed a bit but wouldn't give. The side meant to lift raised only a few inches until it was prevented from going farther by the chain. Still pressing upward, Lone extended his gun arm until he had the muzzle of his Colt only an inch or two from the chain. "All I have to do is weaken just one link enough to ..." he grated. Once again it took two shots. But a moment after the second one the chain separated with a metallic screech before rattle-slapping back against the rising door.

And then Lone straightened his legs with a great exhalation of breath and the cellar lid was hurled wide open. The rain came pouring down onto him and the girls came clambering up around him.

They found the horses—including three extra mounts brought in anticipation of rescuing the girls—where they'd left them in a stand of trees and brush about twenty yards behind the hotel. When they reached the animals, Lone said, "Okay. I reckon you sisters know how to get to the Walburn farm. There are people waitin' there for you."

"Aren't you two coming with us?"

Lone shook his head. "No. We got work to finish here."

"We'll be along soon," Velda assured the girls. "Until then, like McGantry said, you'll find others you know. Mrs. Walburn, Mrs. Doyle—and also Billy."

"Billy's there?" asked the sister who, by the interest she'd shown several times now, had revealed herself to clearly be Billy's sweetheart Stella.

"Yes, he is," Velda promised.

"It's a long story. You can hear it all when you get there," added Lone with a tone of urgency brought on by the sound of suddenly escalating gunfire from inside the hotel. "Now hoist your bottoms onto some saddles and get ready to ride hard."

"I – I haven't ridden in years. And, even then, not very much," Hope said timidly.

"You can double with me," said Stella, reaching down from where she'd just swung up herself and now pulling the blonde into place behind her.

Lone took a step closer and removed from his waistband the Remington revolver he'd confiscated after George the desk clerk tried to use it on him and Velda. He held it up to Stella. "You know how to use one of these?"

"I'm better with a rifle—but yeah, I know well enough."

Lone handed it to her. "Just pull the hammer all the way back, point and squeeze the trigger. Anybody tries to bother you between here and the Walburn place, do exactly that...Stop them, don't let 'em stop you."

CHAPTER THIRTY-EIGHT

EVEN PRECEDED BY THE NERVE-JARRING EXPLOSION, REESE and Dutton had encountered no small amount of resistance in the Gold Tip barroom. As anticipated, there'd been the two bouncers who this time showed they had more weapons at their disposal—a pair of nickel-plated .38s, to be exact—than just their fists. Unfortunately for them, their skill at using a handgun fell far short of their experience at using brute strength. The end result, coming in a quick exchange, was that their combined muscle and weaponry was no match for the hot lead counter-punches the cowboys were able to permanently put them down with.

A slick-haired barkeep armed with a pistol and a sawed-off that he pulled from behind the stick proved considerably more threatening and a lot harder to overcome. His use of the long, thick bar for his own cover and the pulverizing effect of his shotgun blasts on the upturned tables Reese and Dutton scrambled to hide behind kept the cowboys ducking and dodging while trying to score with some meaningful return fire.

At the same time, they were also trading lead with a gray-haired stringbean brandishing a fancy new .45 that he seemed damned eager to put to use after all the other customers who'd been in the joint fled on the heels of the explosion. (Later on, it would turn out the hombre was a veteran gunny called Faraday, who was another of Lobo's special fugitive guests who'd ventured down from his room looking to offset his boredom by trying to scare up a card game.) In the heat of the gun battle, neither Reese nor Dutton had any way of knowing this, of course. They only knew he was an ornery old cuss looking plenty at home behind that fancy hogleg with which he was doing his best to put a .45 slug in one or both of them.

The barkeep's undoing came mostly from a shortage of ammunition. He relied on the firearms at his disposal to help quell sudden outbursts of trouble, not for engaging in lengthy shootouts. As a result, he only had the rounds already contained in the pistol and four back-up loads for the shotgun. Even at that, the fool probably could have surrendered and stayed alive. But instead, after he'd emptied the pistol and was down to only one shot left in each barrel of the shotgun, he decided to charge out from behind the bar and attempt an unexpected head-on rush meant to cut down the cowboys with the final blasts from his gut shredder.

It was a bold move and it did catch Reese and Dutton by surprise—but not so much that it slowed their trigger fingers sufficiently to keep them from being the ones who did the cutting down. What was more, when their slugs halted the barkeep's rush and sent him into a death spin, an inadvertent discharge of his shotgun went sideways and caught enough of Faraday to knock him out from behind his cover. Wounded and stunned, the old gunny tried to still keep fighting but the cowboys shifted their aim and ended it for him, too.

The barroom thus cleared, Reese and Dutton had paused long enough to reload their guns and settle their nerves a bit with a couple jolts from a bottle amazingly left standing undisturbed atop the bar. That done, they were ready to leave the tendrils of powder smoke still hanging in the air and head out to the lobby where they hoped to meet back up with Lone and Velda.

In a case of bad luck and worse timing, however, they emerged from the barroom exactly as Dekker and the three hardcase fugitives were reaching the bottom of the open staircase in the center of the lobby.

THE SHOOTOUT that instantly ensued between Reese and Dutton and the men coming off the stairs accounted for the new surge of gunfire Lone had heard when he and Velda had been sending the rescued girls to safety. The fact that it continued to rage after the girls were on their way made it clear the two cowboys inside must be encountering a tougher time than expected. Rushing to their aid then became the new focus for Lone and Velda.

But that, too, ran into another wave of bad luck and timing.

As Lone and Velda broke from the clump of trees, leaving their remaining horses still tied, Lobo and Gilby —having worked their way up the back alleys of Center Street bent on reaching Lobo's prized hotel and his equally prized Sarina—came around the rear corner of the Gold Tip on its dining room side. On their approach, they also had heard the sound of the shooting taking place in the front lobby so had opted to swing around to the back and enter through the kitchen...Which bought them face to face, though the gloom of the still pouring rain, with Lone and Velda headed toward the same entry point.

That first moment of eye contact was enough to tell Lone with an instinctive certainty he was looking at none other than Lobo Hines. For Lobo, based on the descriptions he'd heard, recognition also came quickly. Causing his lips to immediately peel back in a sneer as he exclaimed, "You two! So you're behind all of this!"

With his weapons already drawn—Tubby's sawed-off in his left hand, his own Colt Lightning in his right—Lobo didn't hesitate to get off the first shot with the Colt. But his rage and eagerness made it too hurried, and the round cut high between the heads of Lone and Velda. This gave them time to react with evasive moves and grabs for their guns.

Gilby was caught standing partly behind his boss and had to shift to one side in order to draw and attempt some shooting of his own. But he was too slow at clearing leather and his side step only served to more fully expose him even as Lobo was ducking back around the corner of the building. From the crouch he'd dropped into as he skinned his .44, Lone fanned three rapid-fire shots and every one pounded into the hapless Gilby, knocking him flat and lifeless.

As she skidded for cover behind an old wooden wheelbarrow that lay on its side about a dozen feet short of the kitchen door, Velda snapped off a pair of shots that hurried Lobo's retreat around the corner but unfortunately only splintered wood and failed to hit the man. Still, it kept him pinned back long enough for Lone to also scramble in behind the wheelbarrow.

As the two of them hurriedly replaced spent cartridges, Lone said breathlessly, "That was Lobo. I don't know if he's got any more men with him but, either way, this wheelbarrow makes damn slim cover."

"I didn't have much to choose from," Velda snapped defensively.

"Not sayin' you did, just statin' a fact," Lobo grated. "Here's another: It's clear from the sound of it that Reese and Dutton need some help on the inside. So when I start shootin' again to keep Lobo pinned back and give you cover, you bolt to make it in there with 'em."

"What about you?"

"I'll join you as soon as I finish out here with the boss Wolf. Now get ready... Knock on it!"

With that command, Lone leaned out slightly at one end of the wheelbarrow and began pouring lead at the building corner behind which Lobo had ducked. He skimmed the corner tight, spacing his shots, holding them at about four feet above the ground. As soon as he stated shooting, Velda was on her feet and running in long strides, making for the rear entry of the hotel kitchen. Lone didn't look her way, just concentrated on where he was placing his shots. The sound of the door slapping shut behind her came just ahead of his sixth trigger pull.

His Colt now emptied, Lone dropped fully back behind the wheelbarrow. This time, instead of promptly reloading the .44, he returned it to its holster and reached to the small of his back to pull, from where it was tucked behind his belt, the Smith & Wesson "Baby

Russian" .38 he packed on occasions where he figured some additional quick firepower might be called for. This circumstance certainly fit. What was more, if Lobo was paying attention, he should have counted the number of shots Lone had fired and rightfully concluded he'd emptied his cylinder and thereby provided an opening.

It almost worked out that way. Almost.

Yes, Lobo came back around the corner thinking he had an advantage to seize. Trouble was, he came looking to seize it not with his handgun as expected, but rather with the sawed-off Lone never realized he also had in his possession.

Firing from the hip, Lobo released the twelve-gauge load from one barrel at close enough range to batter hell out of the weathered old discarded wheelbarrow. Strips of cracked, graying wood were blown loose and sent flying like they'd been tossed into a strong wind. Lone rolled away with a yelp of surprise and pain as sharp splinters stabbed into the side of his face and back of his neck. He kept rolling, seeing that another blast like that would remove any value the wheelbarrow had as cover by turning it to nothing but a pile of splinters.

Scrambling wildly, he made for the fieldstone base erected around a tall water pump with its curved pumping handle thrust out like an arm warning him to stay back. The stones were piled merely a couple feet high, providing only limited cover, but they were the closest choice Lone had. As he clawed to reach them, Lobo's second barrel roared and the ripping load it discharged tore a deep, foot-long gouge just an inch behind the former scout's digging heels.

Rolling from his belly onto his left shoulder, Lone scooched the rest of the way in behind the piled stones. At the same time, he raised the Baby Russian clenched in his right fist. And here was where the recklessness he'd initially been counting on from Lobo finally paid off...Thinking he now had Lone cowering, still with an empty gun, the Wolf boss discarded the spent shotgun and pushed forward from the corner of the building once again pulling his Colt Lightning.

"Now, you horse-thieving sonofabitch, I finally got you!" he bellowed.

Pushing up on his left elbow, Lone extended his right arm and fired two .38 slugs from the Baby Russian into the base of Lobo's throat. The Wolf boss was stopped short, rocked back on his heels. He teetered like that for a couple seconds, a look of astonishment on his face. Then he dropped to his knees and a moment later flopped forward onto his chest and face and was still.

"Not quite," Lone muttered. A moment later he pushed wearily to his feet. The kitchen door looked twenty miles away. But there were still shots coming from the other side and he'd sent Velda in there. He had to go after her.

CHAPTER THIRTY-NINE

Having slipped in through the kitchen and worked her way across the back side of the dining room, Velda eased up to the edge of the doorway opening out to the lobby. Peering cautiously around, she quickly saw that Reese and Dutton were indeed having a tough time of it. They'd managed to whittle down the four-to-one odds against them by one, but in the process Dutton had taken what looked like a pretty serious hit to his shoulder. He was sagged just back around the corner of the opposite doorway, the one leading to the barroom. He was still returning some fire, but his shots were increasingly erratic due to weakness settling in from blood loss.

Reese, feisty as ever, was throwing lead and spewing curses from behind one of two large upholstered couches placed in the middle of the lobby for guests to relax on. The old cowboy was doing anything but relaxing. In fact, the couch was being systematically battered and torn to shreds by incoming rounds from the remaining three hardcases positioned in a semicircle around the perimeter of the room. Their bullets had blown away two of the couch's legs, leaving it tilted precariously, and ripped open the cushions and back rest in so many places it looked like they were vomiting their stuffing.

Velda took all of this in in a quick scan. From her vantage point, she had a clear angle on two of the hardcases—one off to her right, who was shooting from behind the check-in desk; another who was almost straight ahead, crouched behind the stone base of a statue depicting a veteran old prospector with a pickaxe resting on one shoulder. Velda couldn't help notice that, either from some prior mishaps or maybe as recently as from the bullets presently filling the air, the work had suffered numerous chips and dings including both the prospector's nose and one tip of his pickaxe being broken off. But what riveted her attention far more than the condition of the statue was the identity of the man crouching at its base. When he turned his head to shout something over to the man behind the check-in desk, his profile was unmistakable. Velda had studied it too often on the Wanted poster she carried. It was Turk Mitchum.

An ice cold sensation ran through Velda, causing her to catch her breath and hold totally still for several beats. Then, exhaling raggedly, she fought the urge to go ahead and waste no more time putting a bullet in the man she'd been so intent on hunting down. But before doing that she needed to consider the overall situation.

Taking out Mitchum would be easy, he was right in front of her. But if she shot him first, what would that mean for her chances at the other two hardcases? She already had a poor angle on the one off to her left, hiding behind a thick support pillar over near the front door. If he saw Mitchum go down, he'd make himself all the more elusive to her. And the same might be true for the one behind the check-in desk; by the time Velda tried swinging her aim to him after plugging Mitchum, he'd possibly have time to scramble around behind the end of the desk where she'd no longer have a clear shot at him.

So the way to play it was for her to first shoot the one behind the check-in desk and then swing to Mitchum. With the latter right in front of her, he'd have no way to react that would take him out of her line of fire. That would leave the one over by the door. He might be a little harder to root out, but with Velda and Reese both concentrating on him, his chances would turn mighty slim.

With that plan set firm in her mind, Velda took a short breath, held it, then leaned around the edge of the doorway and shot the hardcase behind the desk. Her slug entered at the temple, blew a mist of blood and gore out the other side. The man's shoulders shrugged on impact, his face dropped loosely forward onto the top of the desk. Then his knees buckled and he slid slowly to the floor.

Before he'd crumpled all the way down, Velda was adjusting her aim. She pivoted forty-five degrees to her left and brought her .44 to bear directly on Mitchum. He wheeled full around at the sound of the shot coming from behind him, a look of shock and fright on his face. Velda erased that look by sending two slugs straight to the middle of it. Mitchum's head snapped back, he flung his arms wide, and flew backward against the statue with such force that he caused it to tip and go crashing to the floor with him sprawling on top of the rubble.

The remaining hardcase made no attempt to find better cover or try continuing the fight at all. He simply shoved away from the pillar and bolted for the door. But Reese wasn't having any of that. He rose up behind his battered couch and stopped the runner with one shot. The man's momentum carried him forward for a couple staggering steps and one hand at the end of a desperately outstretched arm actually closed for a moment on the doorknob. But then it slipped off lifelessly and dropped to the floor with the rest of him.

The lobby turned suddenly very quiet.

Velda heard footfalls moving through the dining room behind her but felt no alarm. Somehow she knew it would be Lone.

He stepped up close and put a hand on her shoulder. "You okay?"

She nodded. "Yes. It's over...Except for Dutton across the way. He needs some attention, he's been wounded."

"It ain't so bad," Dutton argued from across the room. "I got it tied off with a bandanna and the bleeding's mostly stopped."

"Maybe so. But don't be stupid on top of bein' wounded," barked Reese. "Sounds like things have quieted down out in the town, too. So I'm going to fetch that doc."

As he headed for the door, Lone called after him, "Quiet don't necessarily mean safe. Stay sharp out there."

Reese waved a hand as he went out the door, signaling he'd gotten the message.

Once he was gone, Lone and Velda started over to try and make Dutton as comfortable as they could until the doctor arrived. Lone paused, looking down at the sprawled body of Turk Mitchum. "I see you got your man," he said.

Velda nodded. "Yeah. I got my man, you got your horse...But it sure wasn't as simple as it sounds, was it?"

As they were passing in front of the open staircase, a sound from higher up on the steps halted them. They turned toward it with drawn guns.

Three quarters of the way up the stairs stood two women. The young blonde they had previously known as Hope Hightower was a couple steps lower than a tall, elegant beauty with piled dark hair. Both stood with arms hanging loosely at their sides and stunned expressions on their faces.

Haltingly, the blonde said, "Are – are they all dead?"

"No other word for it," Lone told her.

The blonde's chin quivered. "Is that my Mel...over by the door?"

"Don't know how he was called. But he's still dead, by any name."

The blonde sank down on the steps, put her face in her hands, and began to sob openly.

The elegant woman, who obviously had to be Sarina, continued to stand tall. Her gaze was fixed on some point out over and beyond the heads of Lone and Velda, as if looking at some faraway thing only she could see. Quietly, she asked, "And Lobo?"

"Him too," Lone answered. "He's out back. He choked on his eagerness to try and kill me."

Sarina stood motionless for several beats. Then, suddenly and unexpectedly, she raised the derringer she had been holding unseen in the folds of her dress, put it in her mouth, and triggered both barrels at once.

EPILOGUE

Two days had passed since Lobo and his Gun Wolves had been scoured from the town of Pickaxe, along with the menace they posed to the whole surrounding area. The rain had stopped, the bloodshed was over.

When Reese returned to the hotel with Dr. Gaines, they were also accompanied by Walburn and Doyle and several others, including a revived though somewhat groggy Reverend Hightower, all eager to report that the town was secured. Thanks to the help of several shopkeepers and particularly to the devastating accuracy of Simon and his Big Fifty, the last two Gun Wolves had fallen in the saloons where they were holed up. There were two other wounded men besides Dutton but, remarkably, there was no loss of life in the ranks of those who'd risen up on the side of right.

That still left things to be resolved, burying to be done, and healing to begin. It would take time. But for the first time in a long while, the area had a strengthened hope for the future.

The army had been notified to keep an eye on

Toneka, the would-be renegade. And the marshal from Lusk was on his way to identify the dead fugitives from the Gold Tip who had payable bounties on their heads.

With all of this either settled or on track to be, Lone began feeling restless and anxious to be on his way. He'd been spending too much time amidst too many people lately, he needed to find some breathing room.

The only thing giving him pause was Velda.

When they finally had the chance to sit quietly by themselves and talk some, she cut right to it. "You're starting to feel fiddle-footed, aren't you?"

The term made him grin. "If you want to call it that...You see, I was on my way to take care of something when all of this started. That something is still there."

"Uh-huh. Something...or someone? Like maybe a girl?"

That made his eyebrows lift.

Now Velda grinned. "You being you, you never said anything direct of course. But there were a few hints here and there... Serious?"

"I don't know. That's what I owe it to both of us to find out. We sorta left things hangin', on account of I had other matters I had to go take care of. Now that they're out of the way ..."

Things went quiet between them for a minute or so.

Until Velda said, "I'll be sticking around here until that marshal from Lusk shows up. I decided I'm going to take the bounty on Mitchum. Any other bounty payouts I'll hand over to Doc Gaines and have him put the money toward the good of the town."

"Mighty decent of you. He's a good man, he'll put it right," Lone said.

Velda regarded him. "What we've been through these past few days together, McGantry, has hardly been what anybody would call pleasant. But having you there...Well, I'm glad you were."

Lone met her gaze. "Right back at you, ma'am."

Later, as dusk was settling, he went around and said some goodbyes.

In the morning, before first light, he saddled up Ironsides and rode out for Fort Collins.

A LOOK AT DANGEROUS TRAILS: COLLECTED WESTERN ADVENTURES

PEACEMAKER AWARD-WINNING AUTHOR WAYNE D. DUNDEE DELIVERS ANOTHER MEMORABLE COLLECTION OF THE OLD WEST FILLED WITH TURBULENT EMOTIONS, POIGNANCY AND TONS OF NAIL-BITING ACTION.

From the Oregon Trail to the Civil War this collection of western adventures will take you on a non-stop journey! Blood will be spilled, lives will be lost, fresh wounds will be inflicted ... but the chance to heal old ones is what will keep everyone pushing forward.

"As usual, Dundee's writing is tough and well-paced. He's one of the best storytellers in the business." – **James Reasoner**

Dangerous Trails: Collected Western Adventures includes: Trail Justice, Trail Revenge, By Blood Bound, The Fugitive Trail and seven novellas.

AVAILABLE NOW

ABOUT THE AUTHOR

Wayne D. Dundee is an American author of popular genre fiction. His writing has primarily been detective mysteries (the Joe Hannibal PI series) and Western adventures. To date, he has written four dozen novels and forty-plus short stories, also ranging into horror, fantasy, erotica, and several "house name" books under bylines other than his own.

Dundee was born March 24, 1948, in Freeport, Illinois. He graduated from high school in Clinton, Wisconsin, 1966. Later that same year he married Pamela Daum and they had one daughter, Michelle. For the first fifty years of his life, Dundee lived and worked in the state line area of northern Illinois and southern Wisconsin. During most of that time he was employed by Arnold Engineering/Group Arnold out of Marengo, Illinois, where he worked his way up from factory laborer through several managerial positions. In his spare time, starting in high school, he was always writing. He sold his first short story in 1982.

In 1998, Dundee relocated to Ogallala, Nebraska, where he assumed the general manager position for a small Arnold facility there. The setting and rich history of the area inspired him to turn his efforts more toward the Western genre. In 2009, following the passing of his wife a year earlier, Dundee retired from Arnold and began to concentrate full time on his writing.

Dundee was the founder and original editor of Hardboiled Magazine.

His work in the mystery field has been nominated for an Edgar, an Anthony, and six Shamus Awards from the Private Eye Writers of America.

CPSIA information can be obtained
at www.ICGtesting.com
Printed in the USA
LVHW041644180522
719025LV00014B/475